BLOOD AT DAWN

DARK INK TATTOO
BOOK FIVE

CASSIE ALEXANDER

INTRODUCTION & CHARACTER ART

Jack: You would think that rescuing my boss and helping deliver her happily-ever-after would earn me a few points with Karma, or at least a couple nights off, but luck has never been on my side. I've got to make my own way in this new reality: my Mistress is dead, but Maya needs help fighting off other vampire gangs, a sacred warrior is after me for my part in their partner's death, I've got a bloodslave following me like a pup, Francesca is breathing down my neck, the Dark Ink staff are in revolt, and the perpetual temptation of Zach is right next door. Oh, and Paco's going to become a vampire in three nights.

I guess no good deed goes unpunished. Especially when you're already dead.

Welcome to Dark Ink Tattoo, where needles aren't the only things that bite...

Dark Ink Tattoo is a scorching paranormal in the vein of Sons of Anarchy, with strong sexual situations and bisexual MCs.

Content warnings can be found on cassiealexander.com.

CHAPTER ONE
JACK

I woke up in my coffin with Paco's hair tickling my cheek.

Waking up in the same coffin as my currently dead best friend and lover was awkward—and it would only get worse when in three days he woke up too. I hadn't gotten a chance to ask his permission before turning him into a vampire. It'd been that or watch him die, and I'd acted without thinking. I knew he'd wake up hungry—I could only hope he wouldn't wake up mad.

I kissed the back of his neck and rose up to Sugar's meowing. "I know, I know, I hear you." I swung one leg over the partition that kept the sleeping dead like me safe from tiny carnivores like her. She wound through my legs on my way to the kitchen. "I know," I repeated, pouring out a bowl of food. "It must be scary when I die every morning, huh? You must wish you had opposable thumbs." She purred while she ate, a sound that was charming even if it wasn't melodious. I was leaning down to scratch her behind her ears when the doorbell rang.

I tensed. Who was left in town that knew where I lived? I'd already made plans via text with the Dark Ink Tattoo crew to meet tonight. Angela and Mark were gone by now, Paco was in my bedroom already, and Zach and Nikki I'd both slept with last night. Nikki had left a bra behind as an excuse to come back, but I was sure she had pride, she would bide her time before calling for it. Zach, however, lived in my apartment complex—and had gotten used to getting lucky. He was also the only one of my recent lovers who didn't know I was a vampire—needed to cut him loose for his own safety. The doorbell rang again, followed by an impatient knock.

"Look," I said, swinging the door open, ready to say something drastic. But it wasn't Zach, it was a woman, the same one who'd brought me the news of Paco's torture last night. "You," I said, letting my voice fall.

"Me," she said, giving me a nervous smile. "I'm Luna. And you're—"

"Angry," I cut her off.

She fidgeted, clearly nervous. "May I come in?"

"No." I stepped back into my apartment and closed the door.

I SHOWERED and pulled on the most business appropriate clothing I had; a white t-shirt, a blue button-down with a crisp collar, jeans that were a solid deep blue, and black cowboy boots. Paco would've been proud of me if he were currently alive, he was by far the more dapper of the two of us. I slicked my hair back and tried my best to give the bathroom mirror a business face. It was hard. I was used to doing whatever the hell I wanted to, which included not taking work very seriously.

But that was changing tonight. Before Angela had left she'd given me Dark Ink Tattoo—Las Vegas's only 24/7 tattoo parlor. It was the perfect cover for a vampire who could feed on sex or blood. I loved doing tattoos, I got to work nights, and the clientele was often interested in seeing the non-tattoo side of me after hours. Being the giving sort, I did my best to never leave anyone disappointed. But if I wanted to keep it going I needed to step up—which meant facing eight to twelve probably pissed-off tattoo artists shortly.

They'd been out of work ever since Angela had closed up shop a few days ago to deal with her werewolf problems. I'd helped her survive and we'd consummated years of mutual lust in one glorious night. But she was gone now, leaving me with an emptiness that was different from my normal hunger. I didn't have many long-term people in my life—being a vampire was, in general, too dangerous. And while being with Angela had been magnificent—and I would never forget the taste of her blood—I knew I'd only just started missing her. She'd been a rare constant presence in my life, such as it was. Someone who trusted me, and whom I could trust. *An actual friend.*

I couldn't begrudge her her new life though. She had a son—and a far more appropriate human boyfriend, Mark. They were probably halfway across the globe now, which was where they belonged, having a normal life.

I, on the other hand, was abnormal—and I'd made Paco match me.

I fought the urge to return to my bedroom and look at him again. I loved him too, in my own way—I always had, ever since our first desperate fuck, after he'd first come on to me in that crowded club. He'd been my first time with another man. And if he left me after this as Angela had—I couldn't bear to think about it now, my eternity stretching on alone, with no one who truly knew me at my side. The thought of it was too frightening—but I needed to go back to Dark Ink now and try acting like a boss.

I grabbed my wallet and the keys to a truck loaned to me from the werewolf pack, made sure the lid was closed on the coffin for Paco's safety, then emerged out my front door—to find that same girl still waiting.

"Hi!" she said, her face brightening. "I'm pledged to you. As a bloodslave."

I looked around to make sure no one else in the complex could hear. "I don't need you," I harshly whispered. "And I don't want you."

Her face crumpled. She was very gothy, had long black hair with straight bangs and oval ice-blue eyes, like a cat's. She'd been in some sort of dress last night, but today she was in black leggings, clunky boots, and a low-cut black t-shirt so tight I could tell she wasn't wearing a bra. A small backpack was slung over her shoulders. "I only have a few hours left."

I pulled my door shut behind me and locked it, ignoring her.

"I just need you to say yes," she went on, following me out to my truck, making me regret the distance to it in the parking lot. "Please. I have to serve someone. I can't be unowned."

I unlocked the door to the truck and sat inside, closing it resolutely on her.

"What're you going to do when he wakes up, huh?" she shouted at my window. How did she know about Paco? Had Maya told her?

She ran around to stand in front of the truck. "Don't make me go back to Maya—please."

"Get the hell out of the way," I said, knowing that even with my windows up she could see my lips and read the look on my face.

"You're going to have to drive over me!" She put both hands on the hood, flashing her cleavage as her chest heaved with intent. "I'm dead if I go back to her." I revved the engine and she started to shout over it. "Bloodslaves can only be free for twenty-four hours! I've only got five hours left to find a new Master to claim me, and we both know if you were going to kill me you would've done it already!"

I wrung the steering wheel. At least it was dark out. An unknown to me neighbor walked by, neck craning back at our scene. I tried to keep a low profile on principle and hoped that anyone else seeing this would write it off as LARPing or kinky roleplay. And I hoped to hell Zach wasn't looking out of his window, I didn't need anything else to explain to him.

"Come on!" she shouted at full volume, lunging into the truck hard enough to make it shake. I leaned over and unlocked the passenger door.

"Get in."

"Thank you, thank you, thank you," she said, settling herself beside me, swinging her backpack beneath the dashboard.

"Who's to say I'm not taking you out to the desert to snack on?"

"Rosalie promised me you weren't like that, last night." When Rosalie had sent her over here to tell me Paco was in danger. Maya and I had murdered our Mistress, and now we were free.

"Yeah, well, Rosalie's dead," I said, gruffly. The girl looked down and put her hands between her knees. "Sorry?" I guessed. I wasn't, really, but I didn't know what else to say.

"I know why you had to do it. Not that that makes it okay."

"She started things, if it makes you feel better," I said. "Where should I take you?"

"What?" She sounded genuinely surprised.

"I'm not in the market for a bloodslave."

"But—you should be. You need one. All vampires do."

"I've been fine so far." I shrugged a shoulder. I'd only found out about the existence of bloodslaves recently—when I'd run from Rosalie after my making, I'd had to find my own paths to blood and sex. Luckily, I lived in Las Vegas. If I played my cards right, I could practically get both delivered.

"But!" she sputtered.

"Yeah, so—here?" I ignored her. "Downtown?" I gestured at the strip malls we passed by.

She turned to face me fully, eyes expressive. "But if you don't claim me, then Maya will." Her eyeliner was perfect, winged out wide. "Would you want to serve Maya?"

"Not particularly. But I also don't want to own a slave. Apart from the ethical considerations, it seems like a lot of responsibility."

She wriggled in her chair. Certain parts of me suddenly woke to watch her—just as other parts of me were annoyed at them for waking. I'd feasted last night on sex with Zach and Nikki both—why couldn't my hunger just leave me be? "Maybe—you could just pretend you own me?" she asked.

I'd been driving to Dark Ink Tattoo out of habit. I couldn't drive past it—I needed to get myself together, to pull my Jack Stone tattoo-artist-extraordinaire and vampire-businessman persona on. "I don't owe you anything."

"I know. But—you wouldn't want to know what Maya would do to me—she hates me."

"That's not my problem," I growled.

"Please," she begged. She caught my hand as I put the truck in park. "I am willing to do *anything*." Her voice was breathless, full of promises. Honestly, everything about her was my type—except for the coercion. It left a bitter taste in my mouth, far stronger than even her being the messenger of Paco's demise. I'd been taken advantage of once and I'd be damned—even more damned—if I was ever going to 'own' anyone.

I pulled forty dollars out of my wallet. "Take this, and walk that direction for five miles." I pointed past her shoulder.

"And?"

"Don't come back."

Her face crumpled and she started to cry. "Maya will kill me." Fat tears rolled down her cheeks, taking her eyeliner with them.

"That's not my problem," I repeated.

Her lips pouted, no doubt holding back curses, as she snatched the twenties from my hand—then crumpled them up and threw them at my feet. "Screw you, Jack!" she said, storming from the truck. I swung out on my own side, watching her go, holding herself with her arms, head low with sorrow—with my vampiric senses, I could still hear her crying and taste the salt of her tears. She whirled around, hair whipping. "I'm going to die—because of your stupid pride!"

Her words hit my hardened heart like a rock. Would Maya really kill her? I wouldn't put it past her. Maya was kind of a bitch, and being trapped under Rosalie's thumb for a century or so hadn't done her any favors. Now that she was free, her taking out her frustration on any other Rosalie-associated targets seemed likely.

The girl, what'd she say her name was—Luna?—was already a quarter of a block away. "Get back in the car," I muttered under my breath, halfway hoping she wouldn't hear. But she did, she stopped and looked back. "I haven't changed my mind. Just—stay here."

"For how long?"

"As long as it takes. Not sure." I recognized Mattie's truck in the parking lot—other artists would be arriving shortly, if they hadn't given up on Dark Ink entirely. I didn't want them to see her with me and make assumptions about how I'd been spending my time.

She swallowed and got back into the passenger seat with sullen silence—and I realized she hadn't taken her backpack with her when she'd left. I'd been played. I ran my hands through my hair—I'd deal with that later. For now—Dark Ink called.

CHAPTER TWO
JACK

Mattie saw me walking up to Dark Ink's and got out of his ride. "Past my bedtime, Jack!" He was kind of a biker-trucker type, wearing a worn denim vest over a black t-shirt, with a six-inch long salt-and-pepper beard.

"Hey, Mattie. Glad you're sticking around." I opened up the front door for us both then paused, realizing I shouldn't make assumptions. "You are sticking around, aren't you?"

"Depends on how late you keep me up," Mattie said, clapping my back with a grin. He was the only tattoo artist I knew that kept farmer's hours, so we sometimes overlapped near dawn. I got the night shift workers on their off nights and he got the long-distance truckers that were trying to get some ink in when they were supposed to be sleeping. "Know if anyone else is coming?"

"Not too sure." I purposefully hadn't looked at the texts the crew had sent me, after I'd sent mine inviting them here tonight. If people were happy to return, they would, if they'd texted me 'Fuck you!' I wasn't going to be able to change their minds—tattoo artists were too much like cats to be persuaded.

Charla was the next artist to arrive. She was a woman like a battleship, expansive in all directions, and the best damn portrait artist I'd ever seen. She was also pissed. "Three days, Jack—some of my clients flew in to see me and I had to work on them in my living room, illegally," she complained the second she walked in.

"I know—I'm sorry," I started apologizing—which set the tone for the evening as other artists joined us. Some of them just wanted to grab their flash and gear and hit the road—others wanted to start a revolt. Angela had texted everyone an apology and a good-bye, telling them that I was in charge until further notice, but she wasn't here to defend me and a lot of the day shift artists had no real idea who I was.

After the carnage, I was left with Mattie, Jacob, Merril, Sasha, Z-Bob, Boy Jamez, and Fantasy. Charla was sticking around too, but her presence had a heavy tone of 'for now.'

"So what the hell happened? I thought this was a solid gig," Fantasy asked. She was a small Puerto Rican girl who knew her way around watercolors—I hadn't yet seen her do a tattoo with an outline and I didn't want to.

"Does this have anything to do with the window getting broken recently?" Charla asked.

I couldn't very well tell them the truth—that Angela had been a werewolf, who'd had to fight her ex-boyfriend who was a werewolf packleader for custody of her son, which she had finally won, and subsequently left town. "Angela fell in love." *With me. At last,* I wanted to add, but I couldn't.

"That Mark guy?" Mattie asked, crossing his arms.

And him, too. I nodded. "Yeah. I think they moved to Hong Kong."

"All of a sudden?" Charla pressed. "She's not dead, is she?"

"No," I snapped. "Don't be ridiculous." I had to take control of this situation, and now. "Look—Angela trusted me, you know she did—I used to babysit Rabbit. I have the best interests of this shop at heart. We stumbled for a few days, but there's enough of us here to get back on track."

Jacob's eyes narrowed, looking around the crowded lounge and counting. "Enough of us to make day shift happen, maybe."

"Let me worry about the nights. I always have." I turned around, making sure to look each of them in the eye. "Nothing needs to change here. Your station costs will stay the same."

"Have you looked on the internet? People have been bitching on Yelp," Merril said, with crossed arms.

"We'll hang up a sign—I'll get it printed tonight—under new ownership. And I've got some ideas about where I can get new clients." The local werewolf pack—which was also under new ownership—owed me.

"Good—because I canceled my appointments for the rest of the week—I thought rescheduling them was better than pulling no-shows," Z-Bob said, eliciting grunts from the others.

"Well, try calling them back. Dark Ink's doors are open."

As I said that, the door did swing in—as Luna entered. "Is everything all right?" she asked.

Mattie gave me a withering look. I knew what he was thinking—that I'd spent the last few days holed up with her, ignoring the shop.

"I'm sorry. It's just that it's already been an hour, Jack," she said, giving everyone present a sheepish grin. Charla rolled her eyes so hard I could almost hear them.

"Yeah, it has been," I said, trying to retake control. I walked over to the neon-sign that proclaimed our 24/7-nature, tugging the chain that turned it on. "So—now I'm on the clock. Your shifts can be the same, or you can renegotiate them with one another. The full calendar's still in the back, by the coffee."

There was grumbling among them, until Mattie said, "I brought the good stuff to restock us," patting a bag he held under his arm. We could all hear the coffee beans rustling.

I didn't drink coffee, but Mattie was a linchpin. "Mattie, if you stay, I'll get you a Keurig."

He appeared aghast. "Keurigs are the devil's playthings," he said. Charla snickered, and just like that, the tension lifted.

"I want Sundays off," Jacob said, stalking back to the calendar.

"Dibs on Saturday afternoons," Merril said. "Except for this upcoming one—and two weeks from now...."

"I don't care, just sort it out," I said, waving a hand in the calendar's direction. As they crowded around it, I let myself inhale.

"You're going to be down a grand a week on rent, Jack," Mattie said, coming to stand beside me, knowing his daily 5 a.m. to noon shift was safe. "This place has six stations, plus the piercing studio. You only have enough staff for three around the clock, maybe four."

"I know." Mattie wasn't the only one that could do math.

"Can I help?" Luna asked, far too perky. Only one of our tattoo artists who also did piercings had returned. Of course, Luna didn't have any art—or piercings—and in Nevada you needed six months on the job experience, plus a half-dozen tests. Still though....

"Do you know how to answer a phone and take messages?"

Her eyes widened. "Of course."

I grinned toothily at her. "Then you're hired."

AFTER THE COMMOTION around the calendar died down, I sent Nikki a text asking if any members of the Pack wanted to book tattoos ASAP, and then it was just Luna and I left in the shop. She wandered around aimlessly, flipping through the flash, staring into the piercing displays as if the captured bead earrings could form words.

"You're just going to stay here," she asked, returning to me.

"Yep. It's part of the job. Waiting for walk-ins."

"What do you do with yourself in between them?"

"Draw, mostly." I'd gone through the stack of mail, sorting out bills. I handed them to her. "These are yours to deal with now. Post office is closed at night."

"So—you're keeping me?"

"I am hiring you. To work here, at the front." I gestured to what would be her chair. "You've got the right look. And I can get Jamez to teach you piercing, if you want, which is a good idea—people are oddly good tippers after you cause them pain."

Her shoulders slumped. "That's not the same as being a blood-slave, Jack."

"It's what I'm offering," I said with finality.

"It's not enough. If I'm not someone else's slave soon, Maya owns me, by default."

One of my eyebrows cocked up. "How do I know Maya didn't send you here to spy on me?"

Her expression curdled into disgust and there was an angry glint in her eye that hadn't been there before—something flintier than the childlike wonder she kept performing. "What?" she protested. I noticed she also did 'affronted' very well.

"You left your backpack in my car as you walked off." Backpacks, bras—I was going to have to have a garage sale soon, with all the items women left me.

"I wanted an excuse to come back!" Her voice lowered. "Are all male vampires this stubborn?"

The bell over the door rang and as we both turned, Maya, looking resplendent, stepped inside.

"Well, well. So this is where you ran off to." Maya looked as surprised to see Luna as Luna was to be seen. That answered that, at least.

"I'm his now," Luna said, running through the hip-high saloon doors to stand behind me.

"Sure you are," Maya purred. Her long red curls were swept out and down, trapped in a net of what looked like diamonds. The rest of her body was hidden by a floor-length fur.

I stood. "Dipping into the family coffers, I see." We hadn't nego-tiated last night after Rosalie's death, so much as I'd just given every-thing away to see to Paco. Which meant Maya had taken control of both of Rosalie's clubs, Vermillion, and the new one they were constructing at the Fleur De Lis hotel, by default. "To what do I owe the dishonor?"

"I need a favor."

I grit my teeth and both inhaled and exhaled slowly. "No."

"The Sangre Rojo," she went on, as though I'd said nothing, "want to meet me. They're interested in purchasing some of our land."

"Our land?" I asked archly.

"Well, technically I'm the vampire who is now mind-controlling the human who signed for it now that Rosalie's dead, but it's mine fair and square."

"I don't see how that involves me."

"Bloodslave, do you mind?" Maya asked, flicking her eyes to Luna. Luna grimaced but then stalked away, hiding in the piercing studio past the coffee pot and bathrooms.

CHAPTER THREE
LUNA

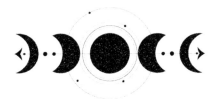

He didn't want *me*?

There were mirrors strategically placed all over the piercing room, and I could see the hatred in my face, in my blue eyes, on every one of them.

I wasn't even *immortal* and I was already a better vampire than he was! I thought about leaning against the door to listen in, but why bother? My mission to somehow become Jack's bloodslave was already finished. The fool didn't want me—he didn't want this—I looked down at my body in reflection. I was perfect in every way. And he thought he could just cast me aside? Like so much trash? When he was the only thing standing between me and survival?

I hadn't bent the entire course of my life to become a vampire, only to give up now. I fished in my backpack for the bone-thing—the nightblade—my new Master had given me. He said it was only to be used on good things—well I had a good use for it, would that count? I imagined myself shanking Jack's neck open with it and me drinking the warm fluid that came out, changing myself, protocol be damned.

But that would actually be damning. Only vampires were allowed to kill other vampires. If I, a human, were to kill Jack, others of his kind would punish me for it. Bloodslaves had to wait their turn in line. No cutting—no matter how nice cutting Jack might be.

The small room I was in was windowless and sterile, with a chair in the middle that looked like it could double as a pap smear exam table. Given that people sometimes did get genital piercings, I guessed that made sense. I started opening drawers and found the tools of the trade—piercing implements vacuum sealed in sterile packages, all sorts of little sharpnesses. I flicked one open, so that the point side jutted out, and looked at myself in the mirror.

I was meant to be a vampire. No—I was meant to be a *goddess*.

And I had been bitten before.

There was no way this thing could hurt me.

CHAPTER FOUR
JACK

"It involves you because we're still on the same team," Maya continued.

"I wasn't aware there was a team." I walked out and leaned against the piercing jewelry counter.

She sank down gracefully into one of the couches in Dark Ink's lounge. "Rosalie was the leader of a significant operation, Jack—a key player on several different fronts. You only knew about the clubs. Do you want to know about the gambling or drug rings?" She read the look on my face. "I didn't think so."

I wasn't entirely surprised to hear Rosalie had had her cruel fingers in multiple pies—the first thing she'd done after she'd changed me was send me in to kill a gang whose turf she wanted.

"My point is that when I meet them," she said, suddenly looking at her perfectly manicured nails instead of me, "I might need back-up."

"Why?"

"To keep up appearances. Rosalie had Tamo."

"So? Turn someone."

"I turn someone, and they're out for three days—plus I look weak. Besides, the Rojo want to meet in two nights."

I pointed at the neon sign behind her. "That says I have to work my shift here, every night."

"Fine, I'll pay you," she huffed, and rolled her eyes.

And if any of Dark Ink's crew found out I was cutting my shifts short, I'd have a full rebellion on my hands. "Why don't you just wait till you're positioned better? I mean, how much more money do you need?"

"When you can live forever, you need a lot." Maya swept up to standing, and straightened the collar of her fur. "Help me present a united front until I can figure out what their game is. I don't even know how much the land is worth—apart from the fact that I'm sure there's still silver hidden inside the old bunker. I've got my humans working on retrieving it, but the Rojo's interest seems sudden. Rosalie never mentioned any other interested parties."

I stood still, and she pressed, managing to shift her face into an almost human expression of need. "I'm asking you, as a brood-brother, Jack."

I tilted my head. "Is that even a thing?"

"No. But it sounded good, didn't it?" She pursed her lips, and then cracked a smile. "Come on Jack—I tried not to kill you, despite direct orders from Rosalie last night. That should count for something." Even when Maya was conniving and untrustworthy—she wasn't all-vampire, all the time, because an all-too-human exasperation tinged her words, a feeling I could relate to.

And it had been Maya's idea to turn Paco. Whether or not that was a good one, however, remained to be seen. "All right."

"Thank you," she said, emphatic. "Two nights from now, midnight, Vermillion."

"You'll owe me," I warned.

"I give payment due on receipt of services—and not a moment before." She put her hands into her coat pockets, and glanced in the direction Luna had gone. "I didn't think you were the owning type, Jack."

"I'm not. I've hired her."

"Uh-huh." A quirked eyebrow let me know what Maya thought of that.

"She says you hate her."

"Well, she's not wrong there. That bitch was always trying to steal my spot."

"What is she like?"

"Faithful. In the same way cancer is faithful, you know?" Maya shrugged her coat higher.

"Are you going to make any claim to her?"

Maya chortled. "Fuck no." I wasn't sure if that was an endorsement or not as she went on. "See you two nights from now, Jack. Don't be late."

"I wouldn't dare," I said, and watched her flow out into the night.

I MADE my way over to my drafting table and settled in, we needed some more flash to make up for the images leaving artists had taken with them. I pulled out a piece of paper, marked it into quadrants, and decided I'd draw a different flower into each. Perennials were perennial—and the flowers reminded me of Angela's lovely English garden backpiece. Our night had been the first and last time I'd ever see it, when she'd been beneath me, me moving inside her, her body bowed before me—the memories made me hard, as they made my heart ache.

And that was when Luna opened the door—no—she didn't open the door so much as she burst in, almost topless, and with her came the scent of fresh blood.

"Did a little research on my phone," she said, shaking it in one hand. I had been right earlier, she wasn't wearing a bra, and her shirt was pulled up high. Her breasts were perfectly proportioned and her nipples hard—because through each nipple was a guide-needle. She walked in, staring at me, and then walked past me, leaning down to get into the back of the piercing display case, bending at the hips so I had no choice but to watch her ass, as she pulled out twin barbells before turning back around. She popped them out of their plastic bags and then threaded them into the guide-needles one by one to pull through.

I watched her, waiting for her to make a sound or grimace—the only tell she had was a slight tightening of her jaw as the widest side of the guide-needle pulled the barbells through, and when she was done fastening them she turned to me.

"Do you like them?"

There wasn't much blood—nipples didn't bleed like ears did—but there was enough for there to be a single crimson drop, gathered on the side of her right nipple. She swiped it up and used it to paint a line down her stomach like an arrow.

I stood and walked over to her slowly, like a man possessed, watching the fire light in her eyes when she thought that she'd caught me—until I leaned past her and pulled a canister of Sani-wipes out. I opened it and tugged out one to hand to her.

"Clean up your mess."

Her jaw tightened again—but she took the wipe before storming off, tugging down her shirt.

I'D FINISHED a sheet of assorted flowers and was halfway into a medley of realistic sea creatures when the front door opened up again and a herd of boys spilled in. Luna, who'd gone back to the piercing studio to sulk, did not reappear.

"Hey gents," I said, coming up to the saloon doors.

"You are open!" one exclaimed.

"Just like the sign says," I pointed at the neon.

"We didn't think you would be—the reviews," one guy began.

"Don't talk to me about reviews, okay? We're under new management now. How can I help you?" I asked, addressing the group as a whole. There were five of them, and all of them looked collegiately sporty in much the same way.

"We just won a soccer tournament," the first one said, all business, with Ken-doll hair slicked back—although a buddy behind him shouted out: "Go UNDERDOGS!" at the top of his voice.

"So what were you thinking of? Soccer balls? Soccer gear?"

"I got your soccer balls right here!" muttered another, to laughter.

The temptation to use my whammy—the power that all vampires had to compel humans—on them and order them out again was high. But even the great Rosalie had bent to the whims of mortals for decent Yelp reviews. "You guys all sober?"

"Yeah—except for Johnny. Who will be, by the time you get to him. This is what we want," said Soccer Leader Ken-doll, pulling out his phone to show me a picture of a soccer ball with a crown. "Except we want all the crowns to be different—"

"Y'all are soccer royalty?"

"Something like that," Ken-doll nodded, looking smug.

"All right. Can do. It'll be a hundred a pop—only because it's a slow night."

The biggest one of them lurched up from the back. "How do we know you're good?" I guessed he was Johnny, from the liquor breath.

"Because this is my shop," I said, sweeping an arm out. I'd always been loyal to Dark Ink, thanks to Angela taking a chance on me, but I had a new and unfamiliar sensation toward it now: filial pride. I gave them all a reassuring grin and between that and the fact that there were absolutely no other tattoo parlors open in Vegas this late tonight, they settled in.

Once I started running my guns—Ken-doll was first—Luna reappeared. She seemed delighted to find people present to hang out with other than me, and she'd kept the piercings in—her tight shirt made them clearly visible.

Johnny started to chat her up first and she pulled him away like a wolf isolates prey. "So you just won a big tournament?" She tilted her head down a little, so she was forced to look up at him through long dark eyelashes.

Johnny proceeded to tell her all about it, from its plain beginning to its exciting overtime finale, complete with kicking motions, weaving his way through the other chairs. The rest of his crew laughed at him or joined in. All of their eyes were on her, even the one I was tattooing—she was mesmerizing. I wondered if that was a side-effect of hanging out too long with vampires.

"Where are you guys from again?" I asked Ken. I couldn't quite tell by their accents, and I hadn't investigated their IDs too thoroughly.

"Connecticut. We go to Royal Prep."

Which explained the crowns—and why they found a goth girl so mysteriously appealing.

Luna waited politely till the end of Johnny's story and clapped in appreciation. "You're so amazing!" she squealed.

"Why yes, yes, I am," Johnny said, leaning against the nearest chair, attempting to sound like a debonair combination of James Bond and Elvis, a consummate player. From the sniggers of the others I figured he wasn't usually like this, not without a half a bottle of Jamison.

"But," she went on, walking among them. "You're not my type. I'm worried you might be a little too whiskey-dick for the purposes of my pleasure this evening. I require a hard man with a condom."

My guns paused for half-a-second—long enough that I knew she'd heard. I only wanted to know what her game was—but she grinned wickedly like she'd scored a point.

"How 'bout you?" she asked, whirling on the nearest player, whose nickname was apparently 'Bear.' Couldn't tell why, he was well-muscled, with close shaved brown hair.

"Uh...." His jaw dropped in apparent disbelief. "I do have a condom—but I also have a girlfriend."

"Dude, this is Vegas, *shut up*," counseled his friend, who'd also fished in his wallet to hold out a condom. He had blond hair pulled back in a high pony, with shaved sides.

All of them were attractive, if you could tolerate the douche long enough, I'd give Luna that.

Luna swayed like she was weighing her options and then with her eyes on me, she grabbed both their hands. "Let's go see what kind of trouble we can get into, eh?"

The blond practically floated toward her, whereas Bear held back.

"Go," Ken-doll commanded from my chair. "None of us will tell. Not even Johnny."

Johnny, who was dismayed to have been passed over, grunted sadly in agreement—and Luna succeeded at pulling the other two forward.

CHAPTER FIVE

LUNA

I knew the piercing studio wasn't the ideal place for a threesome —but sometimes the sexiness of a thing wasn't about appropriateness—it was its inappropriateness, the thrill, the frisson that you might get caught.

We were starting off the night already caught, so I had the advantage.

"Thanks for coming back here with me," I told both of them. They were looking for places to get comfortable and giving one another 'can you believe this?' looks. "I know it may seem like I'm not picky—but I am. I just got out of a long relationship," I said, beginning to tug the bottom of my shirt up. I tossed my hair like a spirited horse, before pulling my shirt fully off. My nipples ached where I'd pierced them—the roughness of the shirt rolling over them and then their sudden freedom made me pant.

Both of the boys just stood there, looking at me.

"Do you need an invitation?" I said, hooking my thumbs into the top of my pants.

"No," they both said as one, and started shucking off their jackets.

Both of them were delectable. I fully believed they'd triumphed in whatever sporting event they'd just won. Their chests were wide, with rolling pecs I could see as they hitched off their shirts, and their stomachs were the kind most girls would dream of eating off of.

"I like that," I breathed, coming up to touch the blond. I pulled my hands down his chest as I leaned up. His eyes were still uncertain, but he opened his mouth up for my kiss.

Kissing is a skill, and Rosalie had spent years teaching me—and sending me out to practice. I twisted my head to fit his mouth better and gently pressed my tongue in. He wasn't eager, yet, but I ground my body up against his, the pressure from his chest setting my nipples on fire, and I played with him, pulling my head back a little, before recommitting and pushing forward, demonstrating the thing with him that I hoped he would do to me, and he gave in in a rush. His tongue pushed deep into my mouth, as his arms encircled me, one of them holding me near, the other hand reaching down to palm my ass and draw me in to him—and I could clearly feel his erection between us, straining, held back only by denim.

I pulled back and looked over at the brunette, the one they'd called Bear. I could guess why now, he was covered in dark fur, and he was watching us with wary eyes.

"You don't like me?" I asked him, pouting.

"No—it's just that," he looked between me and the blond, clearly unsure how to navigate being sexual so close to another man without shouting 'no homo.'

"It's just like the locker room, dude," the blond said. I could almost feel him willing Bear not to blow this chance for him.

"Or like fifteen million pornos," I said, grinning. Who knew, maybe this experience would open up his mind. "Come here," I said, crooking a finger over. "Surely you all have seen this move before?" I said, undoing the top of the blond's jeans, then kneeling.

The blond's cock was perfect, a thick slab the length of my hand. I wrapped my hand around the base of his shaft and presented it to myself like a gift, kissing the tip of his head, then slowly working my way down, watching Bear's face as I heard the blond moan.

"This could be you," I promised, after pulling my lips off the blond—I'd left a ring of dark red lipstick around his hilt. Bear's eyes flicked to the blond.

"Tommy—promise not to tell?"

"Promise not to tell what, dude?" His hands were on either side of my head, fingers winding in my hair, gently trying to pull my mouth back on him. I didn't think he even consciously knew what he was doing, it was just primal.

"My girlfriend and I—we're both virgins."

The blond, Tommy, startled aware again at that. "What?"

"I only have the condom for show. It's like the only one I've ever purchased."

Tommy took a step back, releasing me, standing mostly naked before both of us with the kind of confidence that came from knowing your body was stunning. "Bear," he began in dismay.

"You promised not to tell!"

"Bear...."

"We're waiting until we get married, it's important to her," Bear went on, protesting.

"Bear!" Tommy shouted quietly, and waited until he had the other man's attention. "I've slept with her."

Bear rocked back. "What?" he asked, his voice rising.

"I didn't want to tell you man—but remember last season? That afterparty at Michael's? When you had the flu?"

Bear's hands clenched at his sides. "What? Was she drunk? What did you do?"

"I swear to God she was sober," Tommy said, making a cross on his perfect chest. "She practically pounced on me, dude. Grabbed my hand, hauled me upstairs into Nelly's room, and gave me one of the best blowjobs I've ever had—no offense, lady," he included me.

"None taken!" I rocked back on my heels, watching the show.

"And then after that—she totally snagged some guy from Jaybird's house. Like his third cousin or something, never met him before, never seen him since, but I have it on good authority that she took him to poundtown. That was before you guys were dating, you know? So I never brought it up—but don't let her be telling you that she's a virgin now, bro, come on."

And with Tommy calling fucking 'poundtown,' I had a certain amount of sympathy for this nameless girl. "Look," I said, standing up. "Maybe she just wanted to get rid of it. Sometimes being a virgin pulls all this pressure on you. Especially when you're a girl, everyone wants you to be this pure and holy creature, because of all their baggage and expectations. Sometimes you just want to kick all that aside, and burn it to the ground."

I quite often wanted to burn things.

"There was also Abhrams and Little-T...." Tommy went on, preemptively wincing. Bear's eyes got more and more wide. "Before you transferred," Tommy said.

"Who are you, the sex secretary of Royal prep?" Bear asked, aghast.

"No, I just like to make sure I don't double-dip. I'm always bros before hoes, dude."

They were at a manly stand-off, each half-dressed and getting sillier by the second. I inhaled and exhaled deeply. I could still hear Jack's guns running from the main room—which meant if things went well in here, I knew he'd hear me. "If I didn't want to piss off my boss so badly I would no longer be here," I told the two of them.

"He your ex?" Bear asked, sullen.

"Something like that, yeah," I looked between them. "I am prepared to give you both a fabulous fucking time, but I have ground rules," I said, kicking off my shoes and slinking my leggings off. "Condoms if you're inside me, always. You can ask to change positions, but we don't do it without my say-so. And if either of you say no homo, I'm calling it quits."

Tommy looked over to Bear and shrugged. His erection had

waned a little, but nothing that a mouth, a hand, or a pussy couldn't salvage.

"But—I'm a...." Bear began.

"*Dude.* You don't have to be. Not after tonight." Tommy physically grabbed Bear and put him in front of me. Bros before hoes indeed.

I considered putting on my innocent girl persona again, then decided against it—that was what his soon-to-be-ex girlfriend had worn around him all the time, it'd only lead to confusion. No, I was going to show him as much of my true nature as I thought he could stand.

I grabbed the front of his jeans, setting all eight of my fingers right inside. "I'm not scared of your lack of experience, Bear. Sometimes women like to find men they can train. I only ask that you throw away all your preconceived notions about sex for tonight. This isn't a porn and I'm not made of rubber—but I am completely devoted to giving you a good time. The kind of time most men can only dream of. Okay?"

His eyes went wide and his jaw dropped. "Okay."

"In my house, we ask permission to do things—and we get rewarded beyond our wildest imagination," I said, leaning up breathing the words against him until my mouth was right beside his ear. "Can I kiss you?"

He nodded, quickly. I took his jaw in my hand and bent it toward me, making him fit me, feeling his full lips part. His tongue started see-sawing madly back and forth—I calmed it with my own, and he took instruction readily. Maybe the only thing he needed was a firm hand-slash-tongue-slash-pussy.

"Yeah?" I said, pulling back, writhing my body against his.

"Yeah," he breathed.

"Open up your jeans, Bear. I want to see what you've got for me."

His hands fell to his waistband in an instant, unbuttoning and unzipping, until they were hitched halfway down along with boxers in a school-color matching plaid.

"Can I touch you?" I asked, and he nodded again.

"Say it."

"Touch me—please."

"Good boy." I set both my hands on his chest like a stretching cat and pulled them down slowly, the tips of my fingernails lightly investigating every curve and crevice until I swung my right hand down to encircle his cock. He went hard in an instant, and his hips thrust without meaning to.

"How much sensation can you take?" I stood beside him, body to body, as though we were lovers laying on a bed, and I kissed his neck while stroking him.

"I—I don't know," he stuttered.

"You just warn me then, okay? Friends warn friends—and I want to make this last."

I kept stroking him with my hand, steadying myself with the other on his shoulder as I kissed my way down his body. He moaned and shivered and swayed—I caught one of his hands and brought it up to my hair, which he moved to gather and hold back for me, so both of us could see.

"Can I keep kissing you, Bear?" I asked, my lips close enough that I knew he could feel the heat of my breath on his cock. "Can I kiss you here?" I asked, stroking his hard cock out toward me.

"Yes," he said, his voice suddenly possessive and deep.

"Thank you," I told him, and leaned in.

I kissed his cock much the same as I had his mouth, slowly at first, with just a trace of tongue, working my way up to something more insistent, drawing him slowly deeper each time.

"Wait, wait, wait," he said. I'd been concentrating, enjoying my power over him with my eyes closed and now looking up I saw his face scrunched. I opened up my mouth and carefully pulled back, pinching his tip gently closed.

"Sorry," he said, gasping.

"No problem at all." I rose to standing again. "You want to put that condom on now?"

He didn't answer so much as he responded, tearing the wrapper off with shaking hands. I glanced over at Tommy, who'd kicked off his shoes and pants while waiting his turn.

"What would you like to do?" I asked Bear as he slid the condom on. "For your first time and all, I mean."

He looked around the room. "This wasn't quite what I'd imagined."

"You can always stop." I shrugged one shoulder and gave him a mysterious grin. He shook his head quickly.

"No way. Not now." He took a step forward and leaned in—and I took a step back.

"First, ask."

"Can I kiss you?"

My answer was my smile. "Sure." His lips touched mine and my mouth parted and this time he managed to control his tongue. I ground up against him in reward and his hands wrapped around me, one of them raising to stroke my breast—fingers found my tender nipples. I flinched—but I was also on fire—

"Was that okay?" he asked, dark eyes all full of fearful concern.

"Oh yeah," I growled encouragement, kissing him harder in return. His cock was folded between us, I could feel the rubber of the condom smearing lube all over my belly's soft rise. It wouldn't need it, where it was going—I spun both of us carefully so my butt was against the chair, and then I settled back on it, spreading my knees wide, tilting my hips up and toward him. We both knew it was the perfect height. "Come on in," I said, in a whisper.

He reached down to steady himself and stepped forward, pushing the head of his cock inside me.

"Oh," he breathed, his eyes watching the space where we met, then coming up to meet mine.

"More. Closer," I instructed him. His whole cock slid inside me and I made a soft satisfied sound as I wrapped my legs around him. "That's good, right?" I asked, tensing my ass to bob up and down.

"That's fantastic," he said, his whole body reacting. His hands reached for and found my hips as he pulled out, then pushed himself back into me. "Yeah." His hips started rocking of their own accord, and I made sure to keep my thighs wide to take him. My arms were braced behind me on the chair, and my hair swung free. "Is this good?" he asked, without stopping.

"It's getting there," I answered truthfully, then licked the fingers of my right hand and sent it between us to where we met to rub at my clit, as the weight of his body helped to keep pressure on. I could feel his fingers tensing on my ass, like he wanted to pick me up—I wondered if he could, he looked strong enough and I was dancer light—I leaned forward and wound my arms around his neck. "Carry me?"

Bear groaned—not at the idea, but at the sensation of his cock bottoming out deep inside me. He lifted me up, I could see and feel his muscles tensing—and then he started to use his greater strength to lift me up and set me down again, making me fuck him.

"Ohh," I purred. This was the kind of abandon I enjoyed. I kissed his neck, I clawed his back, I held on while he used me and I delighted in using him, sliding my clit against the flat plane of his stomach every time.

"I'm gonna," he warned. "I don't think I can stop—I need to."

"Do it," I growled in his ear, twisting my legs tight, making him take me as deep as he could. I felt his already hard cock get infinitesimally harder and then—he was shouting, spasming, shoving my hips away before dragging them back on again.

"Oh my God, oh my God," he bellowed, and me coming was a high pitched counterpoint, shouting over him as he screamed, my pussy squeezing the last of his orgasm out of him.

He stood, holding me, shaky and twitching, and stumbled us backwards to the chair where he set me to sit before sliding out.

I regrouped faster. "There. Not a virgin anymore."

"And how," opined Tommy, who'd watched everything, one hand slowly stroking his cock. "If I'd been taping that, I'd be a millionaire."

"Yeah? You think so?" I tossed my hair back to look at him over one shoulder.

"That was like a motherfucking ballet."

"I used to be a ballet dancer, that's why," I said with a laugh.

Bear was quiet, and I returned my attention to him. "You okay?"

"Yeah—it's just still not how I thought it would be? But also better than I dreamed."

"Not every lay is going to be that good, I regret to inform you," Tommy said, coming up.

I gave Bear a wicked grin. "Just remember, when sex is bad, there's a fifty percent chance it's your fault."

"Not when it's me," Tommy said. "Because unlike my friend here, I actually know what I'm doing."

"A real swordsmith, are you?"

"Hand and tongue too."

I gave him kung-fu come-on hands. "Let's see."

"First things first, then," Tommy said, coming in, gently shoving Bear aside. "I'm going to need a magician's assistant—don't go far." Bear shook his head. He was still panting from the effort of fucking me.

Tommy leaned down and picked up one of my feet and kept a hand on my knee as he spread my legs wide, making it so that I was straddling the chair. "While you guys were fucking, I figured out the uses of some things," he said, popping the head of the chair back and pulling out the feet. He set each of my feet inside these, and then took a position between them.

"Are we going to play doctor?"

"Wait and see," he said, giving me a companionable grin—and then he lowered his mouth down.

My clit was still shiny-feeling from my last orgasm—and his mouth sent jolts of electricity through me.

"Can I get an assist?" Tommy asked Bear. Bear shook himself out of his post-orgasm trance and came forward where Tommy picked up his hand and put it on my breast. "Do some stuff," he requested, then went back to licking me as Bear looked down.

"Pinch my nipples lightly?" I asked. Bear did as he was told and I shivered. They hurt, bad, but good. "Gently slap them?"

Bear was tentative at first, but then the sound of him smacking my breasts filled the small room. Each time he hit me it stung, and sent a jolt of pain through me. I started panting, hard—and then Tommy pushed two fingers inside me, fucking me with his hand and with his mouth.

"Mmm," I raced my hands down to keep Tommy's mouth in the same place. "Don't stop—either of you—don't stop," I begged, even as I made it hard for them, writhing as my second orgasm wound up. "Oh—oh—oh—yes!" I let the sounds of my orgasm echo through me, felt each part of me tense and release, tense and release. Tommy's mouth and hand flowed with me, ebbing like a tide, as Bear's slaps became taps then stilled. I collapsed atop the chair, knees buckling inward, hair strewn across my sweaty breasts.

"You think I'm good yet?" Tommy asked.

"I think you're both good," I said, magnanimously. I knew Jack had heard us—there was no way he couldn't. And I knew how vampires worked—I had no doubt his cock was giving him a friction burn inside his jeans.

"See?" Tommy told Bear. "All that and I've still got a condom to spend." He held it up in midair, and I laughed.

"And just what do you want to do with it?" I asked. "Dealer's choice."

Tommy's hand worked his cock slowly, contemplating—and then he handed the condom over to Bear. Bear didn't take it right away, so Tommy started talking. "I mean, if you think you can use it again already and all."

Bear took it slowly, mystified. "You sure about this?"

Tommy grinned at his friend. "I get a ton of play. You have a lot of catching up to do." He held it out even further and Bear took it.

I looked at Tommy appraisingly. "Now that was something a true swordsmith would do."

"Told you," he said with a nod. "But I will be jerking off over here in the corner though, this time, because *God*."

"Who could blame you?" Bear agreed, already tearing the condom's wrapper off.

"So much for the refractory period," I laughed, as he pulled it on.

He looked a little sheepish. "It's just—now that I've done it once...."

"Shhh," I said, hopping off the chair, and motioning for him to get on it. He did so, and I pressed him back against it, kissing his neck and chest on his way down.

"What?"

"This, I think," I folded both the chair's arms in and he was high enough—I swung a leg over him and then went to my knees on the armrests. "Oh, yeah, this," I said, beaming down at him in triumph. My breasts hung free, as did my hair, and it was nothing to push my hips back against him and feel how badly he wanted to be inside me. I lined us up and then pushed just right.

"Ooh." I played my tongue along the edge of my teeth, just bobbing on and off the head of his cock, feeling it fill me and then pop out like a toy. Bear made a pained noise beneath me. "Just you wait," I promised him—and then sank down as I did so. In an instant, he was in me to his hilt and I could feel my pussy full of him. I'd come twice, so I was nice and wet—and also tight and hungry. "Yeah," I said to myself, rising back up on my knees, only to slam down again, my ass smacking against his thighs. Bear groaned gutturally and I heard Tommy sigh.

"Come here, you," I said, looking over my shoulder, as I kept fucking Bear. Bear's hands had found my waist and were pulling me up and down. "Do me a favor—slap it for me?" I asked, shaking my ass in Tommy's direction.

He looked mystified for a moment but then gave me a tentative tap.

"Harder." I wanted the sensation to ricochet through my body—and I wanted Jack to hear.

Tommy slapped me again, while my ass was down and my pussy was wrapped around Bear's cock. I felt it reverberate through me. "Oh yeah—that's good—but a little harder."

This time he waited until my ass was lifted up, nearly shifting me off the chair. I tensed and Bear groaned, feeling my pussy clench as if to hold on. I dropped back onto him, took him deep and said, "Again!"

Tommy hit the other ass cheek this time. I knew I'd still have red handprints in the morning—but the sensations were so worthwhile. "Again!" I pleaded.

Tommy did as he was asked. I shouted when his hand landed, a yelp of pain mixed with surprise and arched my back, taking Bear's cock in hard, while presenting my ass to his friend.

Tommy redoubled his efforts, not by using more force, but by using both hands, arhythmic, I never knew what to expect, where or when. I cried out with each blow, holding myself still now as Bear plunged up from below, bringing his feet up so that he could arc his cock into me.

"Oh my God, oh my God, oh my God," I began, like I was chanting a prayer, and then looked back, and saw Tommy's poor ignored perfect cock. "Tommy stop—come here." My ass was on fire now, I loved it, it'd feel warm for days.

Tommy came up and I reached out for him with my hand and started jerking him off. No—that wasn't fair—I kissed Bear one last time and then leaned over, open-mouthed.

Tommy knew what I intended, and pressed forward, shoving his cock in my mouth without preamble. There'd been a time for kissing earlier but we were past that now—now all of us just needed to come.

Bear held me while I was gagging on Tommy's cock, my breasts pressed against him, rubbing with each of his thrusts—and he was thrusting so hard I was worried we'd fall off the chair, except for when he held me down, hips and ass, his hands tracing over the marks that Tommy'd just left, and Tommy's hips were pulsing, giving his whole cock to me—I heard him groan, felt Bear moan, and all I could manage were the high pitched whines of an animal about to come.

Tommy leaned over and slapped my ass one more time, hard, and it was like he was pushing the first domino over. My pussy clenched around Bear, and the friction of his thrusts set—me—*off*—and I just started incoherently screaming around Tommy's cock, thrashing on top of Bear, my hips rocking wildly into his.

Bear sped up, making animalistic sounds, and then his hands grabbed my thighs to hold me still as he began pounding his load home. Tommy's hands found my hair with both hands and sealed his cock deep down my throat, then grunted a warning. "I'll pull—" he started, but I reached out and around and held him close, gagging on his cock again before he could go anywhere. He made an anguished sound and then I could feel his balls lift as his cum spurt in a salty geyser down the back of my throat. His hips pulsed, spasming, and I sucked out every drop.

Tommy put his hands down over us and tried to catch his breath. His cock had started going soft as I pulled back. "I'm—I'm sorry."

"Don't be," I said, leaning back, not quite swallowing. I knew a little magic—and freely given cum had lots of uses. I ran a finger into my mouth and brought some out to trace a healing pattern around each nipple piercing.

Below me, Bear fought to catch his breath. I ground against him, one last time, feeling him shiver, before pulling my hips up and letting him fall out of me. This condom was just as full of cum as the last one—he probably had years of catching up to do.

"You're...." he began, trying to come up with words for this. "That...." he tried again.

I unmounted both him and the chair. "It was good, right?"

"Better than," Tommy breathed, leaning against the counter behind him.

I looked down at my nipples—I wasn't used to how they looked with the barbells in them. "Do you like the looks of these?" I asked them.

Bear's gaze wandered all over my body. "Completely," Bear said, and Tommy nodded to agree.

WE GOT DRESSED and I sent the boys out first—I didn't want to get into trouble on my first gainfully employed day, so I used the Sani-wipes under the sink to wipe all of the sexy-times surfaces down. There weren't any windows in the room though, so I couldn't air out the sex-smell.

Then I pulled on all my clothes with the exception of my shirt. I looked again at my newly pierced nipples, pinching them experimentally. They were already less tender now that I'd fed them life, so I might as well keep them in. I tugged my shirt back on, and pushed my way into the tattoo corral.

Two of the boys were already wearing bandages, and from where I perched on the piercing display counter, Jack was almost done with Johnny, the third.

"Get down from there," Jack said, without once looking up. I hopped off and pouted.

Bear and Tommy had clearly relayed the evening's events, probably minus the revelation of Bear's ill-behaved girlfriend and his virginity. Upon seeing me, Bear and Tommy looked at me with some sort of reverence, whereas the other three just had hunger in their eyes.

"What?" I asked innocently, shifting my weight to make all of me wriggle, my hips, breasts, and hair.

"Nothing," Bear said quickly, and Tommy agreed, after winking at me.

JACK BANDAGED JOHNNY UP and started mocking up artwork for Bear's turn. I knew he could smell the sex on Bear, my raw scent mixed with his. Johnny lurched toward me, tender on his tattooed calf. "Hey— I've sobered up."

"That's nice," I said, weaving past him to Jack's side. I wanted Jack to smell sex on me as well—for us to surround him, for him to be punished by 360 degree smell-o-vision. I wanted him to know what he missed out on.

I needed him to need me.

"What I meant was, I didn't have whiskey-dick earlier—and I certainly don't have it now," Johnny said, grabbing his crotch like it was a loaded gun.

"That's nice," I said, with a street-wise finality.

"I'm ready if you are," Johnny said, leaning forward—and then Jack was there, standing between us, a wall of angry man.

"Don't touch the girl."

Johnny, not as sober as he thought, was still confused. "What?"

"If she wants you to touch her, you'll know it. Until then, ask. If you dare."

I gave Johnny a look that he knew meant there was no point in asking, but that still didn't stop him. He stumbled forward, bleary-eyed, swinging a hand out at me like a paw through cage bars. "Come on—just one feel."

Jack grabbed his hand and twisted it back and up in a move that sent Johnny to his knees. The other players startled at this and Jack looked at them over Johnny's head. "Did I stutter?" he asked the rest of them. They all shook their heads in synchrony.

"Hey, Johnny—let's catch a ride back, okay?" Bear came in and threw an arm around Johnny. "I'll go with you—we can pick up some more vodka on the way."

Johnny's brain switched gears slowly as Jack let him unwind. "Yeah, sure, okay." He stood and Bear went with him, guiding him through the saloon doors into the lounge outside.

"But your tattoo, dude," Tommy called after him.

Bear flashed a huge grin back at all of us. "Don't worry—I'm never going to forget tonight."

JACK DID Tommy's tattoo in record time and Tommy slipped me his number. I made a silly show of tucking it into my shirt even though I didn't have a bra and he laughed. He knew I was never going to call him and yet he wouldn't be a swordsmith if he didn't at least try.

Jack waited until they were all outside before whirling on me. "You think that's all right? You think that's normal?"

I shrunk back beneath his anger, then lashed out. "You're just jealous because you didn't get to feed."

"That's not it," he said, regrouping, turning away from me.

"It is too!" I ran around so he had to see my face. "I want to feed you, Jack. I want to feed you so badly. And I'm so good at it. You know I am. Just look at me." I stretched out over the nearest chair, arched my back, and threw my hair aside, exposing my whole neck. "You could fuck me and bleed me, Jack. We both know you want to."

He couldn't deny it—I could see his hard-on from here. "Clean up. Wipe down everything. And don't talk to me." He picked up the container of Sani-wipes and threw it short, making it land at my feet, grabbed the calendar, and then stormed into his office.

CHAPTER SIX

JACK

How dare she.

Angela's old office was too small for me to pace in but I didn't want to be out there with Luna. I thought about picking her up and forcibly throwing her outside—or using my *whammy*, giving her orders she couldn't refuse—but something stopped me. It wasn't interest—the animal part of me wanted her, yes, but it was notoriously not choosy. No...it was guilt. As much as Rosalie had deserved to die and as much as I'd wanted to kill her—something in the act felt like it had tainted me. I'd survived for years as a vampire avoiding death, until this past week—and now it felt like death was stalking me. Taking care of Luna was some small way to prove that I was still human—for me to spit in death's eye.

But that didn't mean that I would ever accept her servitude. Which probably meant she'd wisely abandon me in the fullness of time.

Couldn't happen soon enough.

When I calmed down, it was almost four a.m. I hadn't heard the door chime which meant Luna was still out there alone. I went back on the floor when I heard Mattie's truck, and found her hunched over a drafting table. I thought I'd find her asleep, but as I rounded she looked up and then tried to hide what she'd been doing, crumpling paper quickly.

"What're you doing?"

"Tracing. That's what you do with tracing paper, right?" She wheeled and threw it into the nearest trash can. She'd been copying on the flash that I'd created earlier in the night. I should've spent the rest of my evening making more, instead of hiding in the office playing Minesweeper with the calendar, trying to figure out who I could cajole into taking more shifts.

"Next time, let me see."

She shrugged a shoulder like a sullen teen as Mattie entered. "Hello, hello, hello!" he said, in his best Matthew McConaughey.

"Hey Mattie," I said. "Hope you got some sleep."

"Enough," he said with a grin—then spotted Luna. I watched him inhale, then think better of whatever he was going to say. "Any work tonight?"

"Four tattoos. Sports crew."

"Not bad!" The entire building rumbled as Mattie's first client arrived—a big rig shifting into idle nearby. He started getting his guns out.

"See you tomorrow," I said, walking for the door.

"See you tomorrow!" Luna said too, like she was mocking me.

We drove back to my apartment, me staring at the road, her staring out the window. There was no point in attempting conversation, I didn't have anything I wanted to discuss with her, nor did I care what she thought about me. The sooner I got back to Paco and Sugar, the better.

So after I parked, I was dismayed to have her follow me to my door. "Shoo," I said, waving her away.

"I thought you hired me." Her full lips were in a heavy frown and I could see that she was tiring. Just because she'd lived with vampires didn't mean she wasn't human.

"I did. As a secretary. Secretaries don't live with me."

"When I left Vermillion—I thought this was a done deal." She swallowed audibly. "I was Rosalie's favorite."

What I was supposed to glean from that, I didn't know. "So?"

"I lived with her. Full time. I—I don't have anywhere else."

"How'd you get here?" I could make her sleep in a car....

"I caught an Uber."

"And this is the only thing you own?" I said, pointing at her small backpack.

"No." She ran off, looked both directions, and then dove into the nearby shrubbery to pull out an oversized duffle. It was black and the only reason no one else had seen it was because she hadn't come till night—plus my landlord wasn't keen on exterior lighting. "This is. I had to leave a lot of sexy boots behind." She sounded genuinely mournful.

"You staying here—it's not tenable."

"Are you going to pay me a living wage?"

Was Dark Ink going to make any money? Not for a month or two. I didn't know the state of the accounts—that was a job for tomorrow night. "I will. When I can."

"Well—until then," she asked, licking her lips in hope, and pointed toward the door.

"*Goddamnit,*" I muttered, but I unlocked it for us both.

SHE HADN'T GOTTEN inside my place earlier—but now that she had, of course the first thing she saw was Nikki's bra. She stalked over to it like a tiger and held it up to her chest. Nikki's cup size was far more generous than hers. "So this is what you're into?"

"It's a friend's," I said, snatching it away.

"Uh-huh," she said, disbelief apparent in her tone.

"I know Rosalie didn't believe in the term, but I'm managing."

Luna rolled her eyes but didn't protest. "So where am I staying?"

My bed was taken. "The couch or the floor."

"I'm surprised you didn't say closet."

"Don't tempt me."

"Can I take a shower?"

"Sure. Just hurry up. It's almost dawn."

She dropped the duffle bag and disappeared into the bathroom. Sugar came out of hiding to complain at me. "I know. I don't want her here, either," I agreed, knuckling Sugar's head.

There was a rapping at my door. If it was anyone else wanting favors from me I would bite them.

Instead, opening the door revealed Zach. He was still in his uniform. "Hey," he said.

"Hey," I said back. The sound of a shower started as I closed the door behind me.

"I just got home—and I saw that girl—and I thought maybe I shouldn't come over, but then there was a girl here last night," he said in a rush, then admitted the truth: "I park over here now, like a fool, because I want to walk by your door."

"Zach," I said, starting to shake my head.

"I know—you can't give me anything. Your life is weird. There are no promises. But come on now, Jack. If our situations were reversed, would you let a guy like you go?"

I knew *my* truth, and then I knew *the* truth—about me being a vampire. "I would if I knew what was best for me."

One side of his smile quirked up to a grin. "Who really knows what's best for themselves though?"

I closed my eyes and let my head thump dramatically against the door in the face of his logic—and then he was kissing me.

It wasn't just one of those fly-by-night fuck-me kisses—it was soft and hopeful, plush and warm. My hunger sang to be near him—and so did my heart. I knew what this felt like and that it was a bad idea and I still couldn't stop myself. I tilted my head and opened my mouth up a little, letting him push me against the door.

He pulled back at long last. "Can I come in?"

"Only if you promise to take off all your clothes."

"Done," he said, and walked in like he owned the place.

CHAPTER SEVEN
JACK

To Zach's credit he didn't even bother asking who was in the shower. I think he knew if he did, I'd just kick him out, that it'd prove he couldn't handle my 'lifestyle'—if that's what being me was. He just started stripping off all of his clothing, like the obedient sub that we hadn't put a label to yet, but that I wanted to explore. I moved to stand behind him, kissing his shoulders as he went for his pants.

"And you thought you didn't want to see me," he murmured and I grinned, wrapping my arms around him, breathing in his scent.

"Yeah, well, I'm an accomplished liar. I keep trying to tell you that," I said, as he turned inside my arms to kiss me, and his hands started stroking down my chest to find the bottom of my shirt. I pushed them lower instead—I could get my own shirt off—I wanted to feel his hands on *me*. He started working at the buckle to my belt, then the fly of my jeans.

I was hard—I knew he was, I could see it—I licked my fingers and reached in to take hold of his cock, kissing his mouth and neck more strongly, stroking him. My hunger, previously just a match-stick's worth of light, became incandescent, rolling through me, demanding that I feed from him. My jeans were nearly off, I twisted, helping him, kicking off my boots, letting the denim shimmy down, and then we were both stumbling toward the couch.

Someday I'd have to explain why we could never fuck on my bed —but today was not that day, not while Paco was dead there. I pressed Zach down, our limbs tangled, our hips pulsing against one another's bodies and hands and—

The bathroom door opened and Luna walked out, wearing only a towel, surely trying to tempt me. Zach took a double-take. "Is she...invited?"

"No." I took his jaw and twisted his mouth back to me, kissing him hard while Luna watched. His eyes were clouded with desire when I pulled up. "She's going to stand in the corner, and think about what she's done," I said, addressing Luna while staring down at him. I licked against the line of his jaw, waiting to hear if she would follow her instructions. After a lengthy pause, she did, going to the back of my apartment and facing the wall.

"What did she do?" Zach whispered, glancing in her direction.

"Nothing important. Don't get tempted to misbehave—I'm already going to punish you."

I felt Zach thrill at that, his body shiver, his pulse race. I spent my time carefully kissing across the V of his throat, relishing the nearness of his blood, the way that I could send it coursing through him with a touch. "Oh, Zach—the things I want to do to you." I rolled off him, knees on the ground, me looming above. I could play him like a piano. I lunged in and nipped at his nipples with lip-covered teeth, and he laughed and squirmed, sending my hunger soaring. And then I started deliberately licking down his stomach as I brought a hand up to cup his balls, until his cock was millimeters away from my mouth and he could feel my breath across his skin. His breathing had slowed, he was holding it, hoping, as his ass clenched to arch him up toward me—and I took the in head of his cock, relishing in its salty smooth taste. He moaned and I moaned to hear it, as I started working my way down his shaft. His hands came up and were in my hair, and his hips started to rock.

I went with the motion, letting him use me, rubbing the spot just beneath his balls, listening to him groan, feeling his body rise and fall beneath my head and shoulders like a tide. I took an opportunity between strokes to lick a finger—and then moved it back south, to trace a wet pattern against his asshole, before gently pushing it in.

"Ooh." Zach groaned bodily, I could hear it echo in his chest. I used my finger to explore and stretch him—and then to try to reach his prostate. I could feel when I'd found it—and he started calling my name. "Oh Jack—oh Jack."

I purred, sucking his cock deep, feeling the head of it pull down my throat. His hands tightened in my hair and his hips started to buck. "Oh Jack—oh—Jack." I kept incessantly drumming inside of him, and felt his cock begin to twitch in time with my name.

"Jack, I'm," he warned, trying to pull my head back.

I wouldn't let him. I was giving him this orgasm, and then I was taking it back, in full—I growled my dissent and shook his hands loose, as his hips kept bucking his cock into my throat and I pulsed my finger deep inside.

"Jack! Jack! Jack!" My name, and then a chaotic shout as he let loose. His orgasm reared out of him like a tidal wave, splashing down around us both just as his cock stiffened, trembled, and shot cum in me. I milked him with my lips, savoring each wave's slow roll. I didn't want to lose a drop, as the weight of his orgasm made me feel heavy.

"Jack," he gasped, still shaking, as I kissed his softening cock, pulling my finger slowly out of his ass. "Oh—you've got to be kidding if you think I can walk away from that."

I chuckled into his stomach, wiping my lips off on his light trail of fur.

He turned sideways on the couch. "You've got to," he said, pulling for me with his arms. "I need you to," he said, barely able to make words.

I knew what he wanted—to please me. Little did he know, he already had—and it was too close to dawn to keep playing.

"No—I've got to get to bed. And so do you."

He pressed himself up onto one elbow. "You saving yourself for her?"

I glanced back. Luna was still there, still staring at the corner as I'd commanded her.

"No," I answered, truthfully. Zach nodded, accepting it for what it was—not gloating that he'd bested some unknown contestant. With what he and I had, if he ever did get jealous, I'd have to tell him to forget who I was entirely, or I'd have to move.

I rose up to kiss him. "Go home, Zach."

He swung his torso up and his legs down. "Tomorrow, dinner?"

"I'm not the dinner type." I rocked to standing. We were both still naked and as I was in my place, I didn't have to bother getting dressed—but standing put my cock at eye-level for him, and I could see us both thinking the same thing. If I were smarter, or stronger, I would've stepped away—but instead I stepped close, and Zach leaned forward to grab my shaft, holding my cock out for his mouth. His eyes looked up at me as if waiting for orders and I couldn't resist his earnestness. "Make it fast," I demanded.

He concentrated his mouth around the head of me, kissing and sucking, feeling its underbelly, probing its opening with his tongue, while his hand ran up and down my shaft, and his other hand grabbed my ass to hold on. It was like I'd entered some sort of orgasm machine, I didn't have to move, merely stand there and let him work on me. I ran my fingers through his hair and purred encouragement—after fucking him, I was already so hard, I did need to come, we just had to out-race the morning. "Go faster," I commanded, and he did, over and over and over. I started to pant and put one hand on his shoulder, then twined the other in his hair. "Zach," I growled in warning—but just like I had earlier, he didn't slow. I knew as a relatively immortal being that I neither had STDs nor could get them, but he didn't know that, and here he was, taking this crazy, crazy risk—why? Because he cared about me and wanted to bind me to him. My hand clenched on his shoulder and pulled his head in to take me deep as I poured out into him with a groan. His lips and tongue kept working my cock as I had his and it was several breathless moments until I was done.

"That was good," I whispered, looking down at him with heavy-lidded eyes. Dawn was near, I could feel her pulling me the same as he'd been trying to suck me down his throat.

Zach pulled back, looking smug. "Good. I'm glad."

I ran my hand through his hair, and then down his cheek. "You'd better get going."

"Even after all that?" His voice was soft and his expression hopeful.

"I don't let people spend the night—or day," I lied. He looked over to where Luna was, poor forgotten Luna—at some point in time she'd dropped her towel and neither of us had noticed. "She doesn't count, I promise."

Zach inhaled to ask more questions—then caught himself, because he knew they would only push me away. "You're so confusing, Jack."

I walked over to Luna's dropped towel and circled my waist with it. "I keep telling you what I can and cannot offer. You shouldn't hope for more. I'm not playing with you, and this isn't a test. This is how I am."

Zach rocked to standing. "I know, I know," he said, contrite, and began pulling on his jeans. His body was so beautiful, his stomach flat, rippled with the edges of muscles, like the contours of his arms. He needed a haircut, which only made him hotter as he pushed blond bangs out of his face, after tugging on his t-shirt.

"I don't force you to come here, Zach. That's up to you. But if you are here—I'll make you come."

His green eyes flashed at me and then he shivered all over once in memory—or anticipation. "Guess I'll see you around then."

"I suppose so," I said, and went to hold the door open for him. He walked out, and I closed it behind him before I could catch him looking back.

"Master, may I turn?" Luna asked, twisting her head so that her ebony hair cascaded over one ivory shoulder.

"I'm not your Master," I said, throwing her the towel. She caught it—the action made her breasts jiggle. Her other hand tucked down between her legs and too late I scented her wetness in the air.

"I'm so close, Master," she said, and started touching herself, moving her fingertips in high-tight circles. "I could—feed you—so easily—in just a moment—more."

I ran across the room toward her without thinking, yanking her arm away from her sex and pushing her against the wall. "I don't want you to feed me."

"But," she protested. Her expression was completely innocent, and I didn't believe it for a moment. "But what if I want you to?"

"Your Mistress took advantage of me once before. I refuse to do the same to you, even if it's offered."

Her head jerked back. "Freedom is an illusion that I do not need to have! Just because you don't drink his blood, doesn't mean he's not your slave."

"Zach is his own person."

Her icy eyes narrowed like a cat's. "If you say so, Master."

I pulled back, released her, and she regathered her pride. "It is cruel to leave me hungry, too. As your slave, I should not have to suffer want."

"Satisfy yourself—after dawn," I said, and stalked back to my bedroom alone.

I TOOK the lid off of the wide wooden box that sat on my mattress. Paco still lay inside. He looked like he was sleeping—and he looked like he was dead. I sat outside the box and reached in to pet his hair.

Paco was beautiful. Tan, strong, Romanesque, his perfection only marred by the soft scar where he'd been shot once. I played my hand from his hair down to his body, feeling him. It was so strange that he was cold, when I knew how full of life he was. He'd always been smart enough to realize that despite my strength and abilities, what he'd had was greater. Being alive, being able to see the sun—he'd never asked me to change him, and never would've.

Paco had known who I was from the beginning—I'd never had to hide anything from him, like I did from Zach.

And look where my truthfulness had gotten us.

"What have I done to you?" I whispered to him. Only Sugar heard. She jumped on my bed and nudged my knee with her head until I pet her too, before clambering into the coffin beside Paco to hold him before dawn.

CHAPTER EIGHT
LUNA

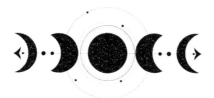

Nothing. No attention. No care. I wondered if the Master I served now knew that Jack was such an imbecile—or how hard pretending to truly serve him would be. I went into the bathroom and cleaned myself up—I was no longer interested in sex.

After that I opened closets until I found one with a few linens and made a bed atop his couch. The room smelled like sex. I ought to open windows, but there weren't any with screens in them—and Jack would definitely kill me if I lost his cat. She was a tiny Siamese, and she came out to stare at me now, sitting and looking at me with accusatory eyes. Why would anyone keep such a small fragile thing? She whined a meow, I was sure it was a complaint.

"I don't know you, and you don't know me," I told her, tucking myself in.

I woke up a few hours later, hungry and feeling sore—more from sleeping on the couch than my acrobatics with the soccer players earlier. I knew Jack wouldn't have an ibuprofen on hand—*why would he?*—or have any sympathy. I was on my own.

I surveyed his countertop, saw his wallet and keys out on it, and had an idea.

CHAPTER NINE
JACK

I woke up and nuzzled the back of Paco's head. It was dark now—and there were two angry girls in the next room. Sugar was easily dealt with, but Luna? Keeping her here was lunacy. I snorted, kissed Paco's cheek, and got out of bed.

Sugar wound around my ankles right on cue, but Luna was gone, leaving only a few sheets folded on the couch. Everything else seemed normal though—even the way the front door was still locked. How had she managed that? I opened up all the closets, not entirely sure how I would feel if I found her swinging inside one.

When she wasn't in any closets, or underneath the couch or bed —I didn't know where she'd gone and I didn't like it. I'd been a fool to let her stay during the day. It would've been too easy for her to do something destructive, to haul me out bodily and throw me into the sunlight. Her hurting me was one thing, but if she hurt Paco—killing him before I'd managed his rebirth—I'd never forgive myself.

Whatever her motives and wherever she'd gone, she hadn't left a note. I unlocked and relocked the door on principle, and got into the shower.

THIRTY MINUTES later I was incredibly early for tonight's shift at Dark Ink—but as the new boss I needed to make a good showing. I swung the door open, heard the bells chime, and who did I see behind the counter?

Luna.

"Hey, Jack!"

She was lounging over the counter like she belonged, wearing a short black skirt with a slouchy neon pink shirt that had a graphic black design. It made her skin look pale and her hair look darker.

"Hello, Luna," I said. I had told her she'd have a job, I just hadn't expected she'd take me up on it. Nor, apparently, make copies of my apartment keys. The phone rang and she darted into the office to answer.

Jamez emerged from the piercing studio, clearly looking for Luna until he saw me. I pretended not to notice and wound my way through the saloon doors. "How's it going?"

Merril looked up from a client and lifted his foot off the treadle for his tattoo gun. "A lot of bikers today." His expression, behind where his client could see, acknowledged that that was odd.

His client, on the other hand, grinned at me. He had leather pants on, but his vest with its distinctive howling wolf logo was hanging from a nearby chair, and his shirt was off. I didn't recognize him—I hadn't gotten the chance to meet all of the Pack during their recent leadership-changing commotion—but if Nikki had been sending him and others over, I'd return her bra to her personally.

"Bikers do like tattoos," I said. "Wolf prints?" I guessed.

"Nah. Girlfriend's name," the client answered, and his grin got even wider. Part of the Pack's recent problem had been their women dying during pregnancy. If Angela and I had helped manage to solve that, Dark Ink would have a steady stream of clients for years to come. I grinned back at him, hoping for the best for both of us, and Luna returned from the office to show me a calendar.

"I didn't know what system you all were using so I've been doing this—if you give me a login to the computer, I can make something more formal, and send out booking reminders to artists and clients."

I surveyed her work. It was full of neatly written names, phone numbers, and email addresses. "Sure."

"You sound surprised."

"I am surprised."

She rolled her eyes at me. Her make-up was impeccable but there were light circles below her eyes—she hadn't slept much. *Human after all*. "I was Rosalie's right hand. You think a strip club runs itself? If you're not careful you get forty girls on Saturday, no one makes enough cash to get by, and you've got shit performers on your Wednesday night." She scooped up the calendar she'd shown me to her chest. "I'm actually good at this."

"I believe you," I said, convinced. "I'll give you administrator access tonight."

She nodded primly, sending her straight bangs bobbing. "Thank you."

The phone rang again. She went to answer it and my gaze followed her. She was the prettiest, tastiest thing currently in the room, and it was like my hunger woke up and opened its eyes. I leaned forward onto the counter—and saw Jamez giving her much the same look. While the *hunger* was a vampire's imperative alone, most mortal men were still afflicted.

Jamez used her focus on the phone to come up to me. "I've been showing your girl the piercing ropes."

"I appreciate that—but she's not my girl." He was a far more suitable candidate for her affections. Lanky, equally goth, and there wasn't an appendage on him that didn't have a piece of metal through it.

"I am too, silly. Whether you like it or not," Luna said, returning, giving me a smile. Attempting to kill me with kindness. I wondered how long she'd keep trying. "I even got you a booking, just now."

"When? Who?"

"Some lady. Two o'clock tonight. Didn't give a name." Luna flashed me her handwritten calendar again. There was a series of question marks beside 2 a.m. "She just wanted to make sure you'd be here."

Her eyes flickered to mine. She alone knew my secret—well, her and the werewolf Merril was tattooing. I hadn't had a choice but to come out to the Pack while helping them and as it turned out something about half-dead vampires was nearly irresistible to them in bed.

"Probably a former client. Wanting to surprise me." I shrugged one shoulder. Over the course of working at Dark Ink for years, I had slept with an innumerable amount of people, and Vegas was a tourist town. It'd be interesting to see who came back again.

"And who doesn't like surprises?" Luna said, before giving me a clearly fake grin.

ONE BY ONE, the evening crowd finished up.

Charla came in and put an outline down on a squirming woman that she practically had to sit on to keep still, managing to do a gorgeous job and earn a fat tip from the woman's husband who, I suspected from their terse banter, had been wanting to sit on his wife for years.

Then there was a rush of lookie-loos, people enticed by the neon sign but who were too afraid to commit—although Luna did her best to cajole them. I watched her work the crowd, killing time with us before their reservations at a newly renovated restaurant nearby. They appreciated the flash art on the walls—some of which I'd just posted—and they appreciated her. She was perfectly attentive, despite her Wednesday Addams exterior, offering them water or coffee, and telling them more locals-only things to do off-Strip—and when they had to go, genuinely telling them she hoped they'd come back. Jamez and I watched her like she'd grown an extra head.

"Did that just happen?" Jamez asked me.

"Pretty sure, yeah." Dark Ink Tattoo was a good shop—but we weren't known for our warmth and out-going nature—unless the part where I slept with clients late at night counted.

"Huh," he said, before heading back to his autoclave.

Huh, indeed. Luna was drawing a map for one of the stragglers, who would've rather been getting her phone number instead, I'd bet. She looked up and over, caught me watching, and waved.

THEN CLIENTS AND ARTISTS DWINDLED, until we were the only two people left in the shop.

"So did you have a good first day?" I asked. I liked what she'd done—and what I'd seen of her in here with other people. I wondered if I pretended to play along, if she'd pretend too.

She hopped up onto the counter. Her skirt was so short, I knew the glass would be cold against her thighs. "It was all right. Different."

"From Rosalie? I'm sure."

She waved her hand in between us, like she was polishing a mirror. "Is this really all there is to you, Jack?" Her nose crinkled, like a bunny.

I sighed. I knew without her saying what she was asking. "Yeah. This is pretty much how I want to be. People like me. I get paid to draw on them with needles. Mysterious women and-or men call up to make sex appointments with me. This is good."

"There's no drugs? Or mind control? Or torture?" she asked.

I stifled a laugh. "Not on my watch, if I can help it. Normal people don't want those things."

Her eyebrows rose. "But you're not a *person*, Jack. You're a vampire."

"And you're not normal," I said. "Why is that? Did Rosalie break you?"

Luna's head snapped back like I'd hit her. "No. Rosalie...I wanted what she offered, so I offered myself to her. Once I'd realized what she was, and what she could help me become."

And here it was, the real reason I was being forced to suffer her attention. "So you don't want to offer me blood or sex out of the kindness of your own heart, is what you're saying. You want something in return for it."

She hopped off the counter. Despite having been on best behavior earlier, and wearing an innocently pink top, now the cravenly hungry Luna I'd met the prior night came back, padding toward me like a jungle cat.

"People pay for things, Jack. There's no shame in an honest transaction. I want what you have. I'm willing to give things to get it. Commerce makes the world go round." Her voice dropped an octave to a throaty purr. I stood unmoved.

"What if I told you that what I have is a curse that I wouldn't wish on anyone?"

She groaned and rolled her heavily lined eyes. "Then I'd ask why the hell you gave it to Paco."

"He's different. He was going to die."

She picked a pencil up off of the counter behind her and held it with the sharpened tip at her throat. "And if I dug my carotid out to bleed, what would you do?"

I stood still, implacable. "I'd go get some paper towels."

She watched me for any hint of emotion and then snorted, oddly satisfied. "For someone who thinks they're so human, you're not." She put down the pencil and behind her the bells chimed as someone walked in.

"Hello?"

It was a woman's voice and as Luna turned I could see her. She was a black woman, as lean as she was tall. Her brown eyes were wide-set, her lips full, and she was wearing a white tight-fitting long sleeved shirt, and a long white skirt that made the darkness of her skin appear more stark. Her hair was close cropped and she wore no make-up—she didn't need any. "Hey—I was looking for Jack?" She had a light accent and glanced between us as though worried she'd interrupted something.

"You've found him." I gave her a warm smile. See? Word of mouth. All Dark Ink Tattoo needed was word of mouth. I nudged Luna. "Go home."

"What?"

"Your shift's over. I've got this. I'll set you up with the computer stuff tomorrow."

"But—how am I," she started to protest.

"You got here somehow, right? I suggest you take that same mode of transportation—only this time in reverse." I could see her transforming back into petulant-girl mode before my eyes, and I didn't want the customer to see. "Don't make me tell you," I said under my breath, threatening her with my whammy.

Her eyes narrowed sharply and her lips set. But she'd been whammied before—I had no doubt Rosalie liked to order even her right-hand-woman around—so she knew what I could do.

"Fine. See you later. At home," she said spitefully.

I nodded and gestured toward the door. Luna grabbed her bag and stomped out. Watching this, the woman's eyebrows rose.

"Sorry," I apologized. "New hire, visiting from out of town—distant cousin. She thinks she's more important than she is. Sometimes you tell an aunt you'll do a favor, and you get more than you bargained for."

The woman crossed her long arms. "I see."

"So, now—how can I help you? I only do tattoos—if you want a piercing, you'll have to come back during daytime."

"I want someone to add on to my original art." She gave me a Cheshire cat smile, teeth white against the darkness of her lips.

"Come on back," I said, holding one of the saloon doors wide.

I SETTLED her into my station and handed her my portfolio. She didn't look like the tattoo getting type—especially what with all the clothes hiding them—but I would do my best, no matter what. Maybe she'd made a bad decision back in college and what she wanted was a cover-up. You had to be confident to tattoo darker skin, to have an appreciation for it, so that it would appreciate your art—and luckily for her, confidence was my middle name.

"These are nice and you come highly recommended," she said, closing the examples.

"But?" I asked, because I heard one.

"But not everyone is used to tattooing on me."

There was a stillness to her, one I had attributed to the elegance that seemed to surround her, but now up close it was eerie. Almost pressing.

Maybe confidence was just my middle initial.

"If you show me what you want worked on, I'll try a sketch. If you don't like the sketch, no harm done."

"All right." She started rolling up one sleeve, revealing a long and dagger-like shape that could also be a cross, in ink done three shades darker than the natural tone of her arm. It was subtle—it made it look like the cross was a part of her, living just beneath her skin.

And I had recently seen a similar tattoo on a dying man who'd sworn vengeance on all vampire-kind.

"That's lovely," I said, pushing back. If she was human, I could whammy her. If she wasn't.... "Let me get my good pen," I said and turned, acting normal while watching her reflection in the shop glass.

The second my back was turned, objects behind me began levitating. My tattoo gun, my tray of inks, even Luna's neck-stabbing pencil. I had no doubt she could hurl them at me, the only question was with how much force. I had inhaled to command her to drop them—even though I didn't know how she was holding them up—when the bells chimed and Luna raced back in, a blur in the glass's reflection.

"Don't hurt him!" she shouted, a battle cry, and in her hand was something jagged and white. As I whirled, objects dropped, and the strange woman darted away, pressing her back against my office's wall.

Luna leapt over the counter and raced to my side, hissing like a cat, and I could see what she held—it looked like a rib-bone on a handle, like a tiny scythe. The woman pushed her hands out to ward it away from her, while Luna made forward jabbing motions.

"He's mine!" Luna shouted. "All mine!"

"That is a matter of debate," I said, stepping aside. The woman's eyes weren't on me anymore—she was looking for an exit—and I heard a nearby window start to rattle.

"*Don't!*" I commanded with my whammy. The rattle stopped, and Luna momentarily stilled. "I'm sorry—windows are expensive."

The woman's jaw ground as if in pain. "What perverse things would you have me do, demon?" Every time Luna got closer to her with the bone she held, the woman winced.

"Luna, stop that," I said.

Luna growled. "Don't get your hopes up. He won't even do perverse things with me." She lowered her arm a little, but still held the bone out like a weapon. The woman stopped wincing, but her eyes gave away that she knew she was trapped.

"I suppose you know Bryan?" I'd talked to the dying tattooed man before his death. He'd been planning a raid on Rosalie's secret hideout prior to his capture. He'd called it a 'nest,' and he'd lined the edges of the tunnels there with C4.

"I knew Bryan," she said, correcting my tense. "Before you killed him."

I raised a hand as if about to swear. "Technically, I did not kill him, nor drink from him. But I'll admit that I was there. I was watching a friend of mine's child at the time, trying to protect him from a werewolf army—I didn't have any leverage to use on Bryan's behalf. I'm sorry." She snorted in disbelief. "He did say something before he died," I went on. "About some guy named Sam. He wanted him to know he'd died."

"He meant Samantha. She who stands before you, now."

And she who had some sort of freakish telekinetic powers. I nodded. "Again, I'm sorry. If it makes you feel better, I killed both Tamo and Rosalie myself. And I got to use his very cleverly placed bombs."

She—*Sam*—still appeared tense. I reached out and pushed Luna back, and at that, Sam began relaxing.

"Why are you here, Sam? What can I do for you?"

Luna gave me an aghast look. I ignored her.

Sam settled her shoulders and lifted her chin, becoming regal once more. "I would see where he died."

I'd left Bryan at the bottom of a mine-shaft—that'd then been exploded. "You'd need a backhoe and a construction crew to get his body back."

"I don't need that. I only need to see where he died."

It occurred to me belatedly that being telekinetic was perhaps like being your own construction crew. "Fair enough. I've got a booking at two."

"That was me," she admitted.

"Well then—I guess my evening's free."

"No, it is not," Luna said, jabbing her weapon forward and Sam shuddered in pain.

"Luna—stop that," I repeated. She followed orders, but only barely, and her eyes were dark. "Sam's not going to kill me, is she?" I asked the woman in third person.

She spread her hands wide in innocence. "Not tonight."

"Give me a few minutes to close up."

Sam stood and made her way outside. Luna watched her like a hawk, before whirling on me the moment the door was closed.

CHAPTER TEN
LUNA

"I'm coming with you." Jack was bone-headed and stupid in so many ways, but he was not going to die tonight. He'd kicked me out of Dark Ink but I'd had a feeling about her. I'd been involved in too many dark arts to not know when some sick being full of goodness had arrived—which begged the question why the hell Jack—*a vampire!*—had not seemed to know it.

"No, you're not," he said.

"Didn't you see what she can do?" Because I had—I'd turned, once outside, and seen the power I'd felt manifested into levitation. She'd had all the nearby objects floating up, like rotating planets. Rosalie had warned me about creatures like her before, all pure and sacred, thinking they were better than everyone else, just because they could walk beneath the sun during the day but they still died.

What was the point in being 'good' and believing in 'eternal life' if you didn't actually get to live it?

"I saw it in reflection."

"Then you know that it's not safe for you! She's dangerous!"

"Show me that," he said, ignoring me as he held out his hand.

My new Master had said nothing about hiding the nightblade

from Jack but I was reluctant to show it to him all the same. I handed it over, slowly. He took it and turned it, exploring every side, trailing a finger along its edge, weighing its handle in his palm.

"Where did you get this?"

"Rosalie."

"Before or after she died?"

I flushed, remembering the moment my new true Master approached me, and how. "Are you accusing me of stealing?"

"No. It's just that it's clearly very powerful," he said—and handed it back. I took it, feeling safer with it around.

"It only works on good people."

"Good people?" His lips quirked.

"You know. The kind we're not supposed to be?" I ran my free hand through my hair and it caught on a tangle. "I can't let you go out alone with her."

"You don't trust her word?"

"Would she be safe from you if the situations were reversed?"

"Likely."

I swung the nightblade out at him. He didn't flinch, but he did chuckle. "Just checking," I complained.

He didn't bother to hide a smirk. "It's going to be all right, Luna. I have something she wants—information."

"And after she gets it, what then?"

"Then we'll part and go our separate ways."

"You don't understand, do you? If something happens to you—what do you think happens to me?"

"I asked Maya," he said, looking increasingly bemused. "She said no take-backs. You're fine."

"That's not the point!" I shouted at him.

What would my new Master do if Jack died? I was on a mission! Would our arrangement be null and void? If I had to find a new master to serve, and start again—the disease I carried might not give me enough time. Every day I continued to live as a human my clock was ticking.

"Luna, if I die, you go back to Idaho, or Indiana, or Wisconsin, or whatever other state your parents are in, being very depressed about your life choices right now."

"Fuck you," I muttered.

Jack snorted. "Stay here if you want, or go home. Clearly you have keys. Do you need money for a ride?"

I looked up at him, biting my tongue, dying to say what was on my mind—*Who's to say you won't come home and find your precious Paco staked?* Would but for my Master's wishes, I'd stake both of them tomorrow at dawn. It wouldn't have been the first head I'd sawed off a body—or the second.

"Here," Jack said, taking my silence for agreement. He reached for his wallet and pulled out a twenty. "You did a good job here today, Luna, and I appreciate that. I promise Dark Ink will pay you what you're owed in full."

That was the only true thing he'd said all evening. One way or another—he was going to pay. For Rosalie, for the disruption of all my hopes and dreams—I snatched the twenty from his hand and stomped outside.

Glinda-the-Good-Witch, a.k.a. Sam, was waiting outside by a red convertible with the top down. She gave me a nod of acknowledgement. I flipped her off and started walking.

CHAPTER ELEVEN
JACK

"Aren't you cold?" I asked the strange woman I sat beside. It was wintertime in Vegas. Good for me, seeing as I got more hours awake, but bad in most other respects—the wind could whip in from the desert and freeze the legs off of even the most determined hooker.

"No, you?" Sam asked, shouting over the wind as she looked over. She didn't have any hair to whip—I wondered what that must feel like, the sensation of air against one's scalp, if it was anything good, like fingernails.

"Not in the least," I said.

We'd been driving for the past forty-five minutes, following my remembered directions. Rosalie's bunker had been a bit off the charts—and I hadn't spent long looking at it after I'd set off explosions and been freed from the earth. I wasn't really sure what we'd find.

We wound past the other shanties and shacks, people determined to live an off-the-grid lifestyle and those who wanted space to make meth, until we reached the final turn that I remembered.

"Go slow. Potholes," I counseled.

"Thanks." She took it down a gear and flicked her headlights up to bright.

Three minutes later, the remnants of Rosalie's bunker loomed. It'd looked like an RV for all intents and purposes—the bunker part had been the underground tunnels and mineshafts it'd been connected to. Sam put her car into park, and hopped out.

The Pack had been by to pick their bikes up from out front. And some of Maya's crew had come by to dig out the guns and silver munitions since I was last here, leaving an open pit underneath the RV, which they'd left up precariously on jacks. The RV itself was half-slagged—it looked like the explosions I'd triggered had set it on fire.

Sam looked over at me. "What happened here?"

"You think Tamo went down without a fight?" I walked up in the light of her headlights and kicked the rubble, remembering. I'd been close to death before, but never so much as when Tamo had tried to kill me. "Your man was planting bombs before he got caught. Tamo bled him out, I killed Tamo, and then had to run away underground from the werewolves who were angry at the time. The only thing that got me out alive was your man's C4."

One of her eyebrows rose archly. "One vampire drank all of Bryan's blood?"

"He also got beat up." I decided to leave Maya out of things, despite the fact she'd been there and had drank from him. "Tamo was a huge fucking vampire."

"So I've heard." She gestured out at the surrounding rocks. "Can you guess where Bryan was last?"

"Hmm." I jumped up to the top of what remained of the RV's roof. The structure underneath me shimmied and that instability was echoed into the landscape beyond. All the land behind the RV had settled down after the bombs, into the collapsed mine shafts below. "I think it's over there." I pointed, and looked down at her. "I'd say it's not safe for a human, but...."

"I'll be fine," she cut me off. "Show me."

"Your funeral," I said with a shrug. She glared, and I jumped down to the RV's far side.

I halfway expected her to levitate herself over, like something out of a superhero movie, but she didn't, she made her own way around the RV, her white clothing bright beneath the starlight. I stood for a second, getting my bearings, then guesstimating where we had been —there was the initial tunnel, and then a hallway, and then the offshoot where Bryan had been. All the rubble looked the same on this side of it. Considering how close I'd been to being underneath it —I shuddered at the memory.

"Here?" she asked, coming to where I stood.

"I think so." I swung my arms wide. "Within a radius of twenty feet or so of here, for sure. Honestly not sure how far down."

"All right. Back up."

I was unused to taking orders from strangers, but I was highly curious. And if she was going to excavate down to get to his body, I probably wanted to be out of boulder-throwing range. I jumped back over a few mounds of earth and crouched, ready to jump again.

She did something with her hands in front of her. It was like she was dancing—or drawing a word. It was oddly compelling to watch and so I didn't trust it—doubly so when it started to glow.

When her hands were moving so fast that the image of what she drew hung in front of her, like a sparkler's stream, she cast it away from her. The glow spun outward and then dropped, waves of brightness rippling out from it as it sank into the ground.

I was unsure what we were waiting for. I hadn't known magic literally existed in the world until recently. It made sense, given that I was a vampire and now I knew several werewolves—but whereas movies and books had given me templates for us, albeit occasionally misinformed ones, I had no guidebook for what she was yet.

The ground beneath our feet sighed. Nothing shifted that I could tell, but I heard a sound as if an hourglass had been turned, and the sands inside it were pouring out. Then a new brightness emerged, in the shape of a man, liberating itself, climbing out of the ground as though it were a door.

I moved closer, quietly—whatever happened next, I wanted to see.

"My heart," Sam whispered, reaching out her hand, and placing it on the bright-man's chest. "What did they do to you?"

I waited for him to answer her. He looked exactly like he did when he'd been murdered, only glowing blue. The cross tattoos on his arms were especially radiant.

She walked up to stand beneath him—he hovered a good foot off the ground now—and walked around him in a circle, inspecting every part. When she reached the front of him again she told him something, too quietly for me to hear, and leaned in to kiss his cheek. Then she stepped back, snapped her fingers, and the image disappeared.

I had done as she asked and she had powers unknown to me, plus every right to be pissed. So I hung back, waiting—and when the wind changed, I could taste her tears.

"Are you all right?" I asked from a respectful distance.

"No. But here I stand," she said. And then she swayed and fell over into black.

My fear almost cost her her life. I thought she might be playing with me, luring me in for revenge, and so I didn't run as quickly as I could —and by the time I reached her side it was almost too late. Her body lay in darkness—like a well of shadow had opened up beneath her, like a hungry mouth. Nothing reflected in it, not the stars nor waning moon, it was like it was eating all light—and her. I grabbed for her without thinking, trying to pull her out of it, feeling whatever it was that wanted her pulling back.

Beneath us both the mouth yawned wider, trying to entrap me. I knew I couldn't let it get all the way under me—if I did, neither of us would come out.

"Sam!" I shouted, pulling. I held her knee and a shoulder, making her sprawl in an ungainly fashion as I yanked her to my side. I jerked her toward me and darkness splashed against my hand, and I had never felt that caliber of cold before, it was like getting shot with ice. "SAM!" I shouted, as loud as I could.

I'd spun her head toward me and was afraid to drag her any harder—I was strong, but she was mortal, and in this strange game of tug-of-war it seemed possible I could pull her in two.

"SAMANTHA! WAKE UP!" I shouted. "BRYAN NEEDS YOU!"

At that, she finally stirred—and as she did, the darkness shrank beneath her, like it was draining out. I stumbled back when it let go of her, holding her to my chest, panting in fear and pain from where the bitingly cold dark had splashed me.

Her eyes blinked open, registered where she was and who she was touching, and her expression changed to one of horror.

"Get off me, beast!"

"You're the one on me," I said, shifting to the side, now trying to keep both her and the thing that'd attacked her in my line of sight. The dark tide was gone now though, everything back to normal under starlight. "You fainted and something came up out of the ground to try to eat you, it looked like."

She rolled to a crouch, blinking. "The conduit—I must've left it open for a second too long."

Her eyes scanned the ground. "And?" I prompted.

"I let something other than Bryan through."

"Did it go back? Or is it still here?" I stood now, scanning the ground, waiting for any and all shadows to betray me.

"I don't feel it," she said, shaking her head and standing too.

"You didn't feel it the first time, so that's not exactly comforting."

She took a step back. "We should go."

"Agreed," I said, and followed her back, eyes watching for darkness.

CHAPTER TWELVE
LUNA

I walked for an hour, the nightblade in my hand, willing for someone to come and try to mug me. I wanted to take my anger out on someone, even if it might mean their life.

When no one did, I put the nightblade away and summoned a ride on my phone. I still had Rosalie's credit cards on file and I'd use them until Maya cut me off. Considering the way she was likely spending, she might not notice—not until she got herself another bloodslave just like me. Someone had to do the real accounting after cooking the books.

I stood on a street corner for five minutes, completely ignored, until a tan Honda Civic pulled up. "Rosalie?" asked the driver.

"Yep," I said, and the driver left it at that, heading off to the address I'd given him, back to Jack's small apartment. I'd already walked halfway there—if my shoes were more comfortable, I might never have called.

I was staring out the window at the receding neon of the Strip when the driver paused and took a sharp turn into an alley.

"Hey!" I protested, opening my bag in an instant. I might get to use the nightblade after all. Then a darkness descended over me, pressing down on me from every side at once.

"I need you right now. Service me." My Master's voice was throaty in my ear.

"Master?" I said, looking for him and finding myself alone, despite the fact that I could feel his presence. I glanced into the front seat and saw the driver staring resolutely into space.

"Service me. Now," he commanded as he fell upon me, pushing me down against the seat.

How many times had Rosalie taken me like this? Without warning, without preamble? I knew better than to fight it, and when my seatbelt whipped away from me and hands reached up the insides of my thighs, I let my knees fall open, helpless against the torrent of his desire. My panties were pushed away as sudden heat pressed inside. I gasped in surprise, to feel taken so—as other hands rushed their way up my top and cupped my breasts, as unseen mouths sucked my newly pierced nipples.

Just like the other night, when I had not known what was happening, nor what I could do, I fell again into the same helpless trance, my back arched in pleasure, my hips thrusting at once, the sensation of fingers—or tongues—thrusting into my mouth, filling me, as electricity sizzled from my breasts to my hips, as my nameless Master's longing and determined strokes stirred everything inside.

There was a mouth or a hand at my clit, rolling it shamelessly with each thrust, as hands held my wrists trapped and still somehow also pressed my ankles down, the rest of me thrashing against the upholstery. I threw my head back, so close so quickly. "Master?" I asked, needing to hear his permission—wanting him to claim me.

"Yes, servant. Go," he commanded, and I did, crying out helplessly as I shuddered. Such pleasures reeled through me, head to toe, and every part of him that touched me followed me through, not stopping until I was finished, panting, sagging against the seat, wetness leaking between my thighs.

"I long for the night I may return your favors," I whispered and collapsed.

This seemed to please him. "Your current form would not survive it."

"Then change me," I pleaded.

He chuckled. "You used the blade. Where is your victim?"

I went still, trying to decide how fine the line between protesting and making excuses this new Master would tolerate. Rosalie's had been as thin as a knife.

"Jack didn't let me kill her." I made sure to sound upset.

"Why not?"

"He thinks her...honorable."

"Tell me," he commanded and I had no choice. I relayed everything that had happened, since I'd seen—no, felt—him last.

"A Faithful," he murmured to himself. I tensed. Rosalie had always been fearful of the Faithful's attention—but they were like the bogeyman. You were scared of them, but never met one—because if you met one, it was too late. "Will she kill him?"

I swallowed. "I hope not."

"And he hasn't claimed you yet," he said, not a question. "Not blood, nor sex."

"I have offered. I have tempted," I swore. "I have been gracious, I have been kind, I have been cruel, I have tried jealousy—I have let him scent my blood." I started panicking. If this creature would not have me, then who was left? His power was real, I knew it, the driver had not turned around, it was as if my Master had stopped time. And I'd felt the power of his nightblade when *she* was around—it had wanted me to shove it into her heart, like a soul-seeking dowsing rod.

"Be still," he said, and I fell to silence. "There is nothing wrong with you. The error is with him. He does not act as one of our kind ought to. He brings shame upon our title."

I could've cried in relief. "Thank you, Master."

"But should he live the night, I need for him to trust you. I need for him to feel bound to you. I need him to be obligated." I felt a pressure glide down my cheek—and then stroke to the nape of my neck. "Create a situation if you must. Give him no choice."

"Yes, Master," I said, as an unseen hand circled my throat like a collar.

"You must show him your pleasures, Luna. Bind him to you—or else."

Or else what? I wanted to know—but I knew from experience it was never a good idea to ask.

"How else can I serve you?" I asked, knowing he could feel the thrill of my heartbeat. "Or might I serve you again, as I already have?"

He made an agreeable sound and I felt the weight of his presence nearing, then he paused. "A more tempting morsel awaits," he said —and he was gone.

He hadn't even dismissed me. He'd just disappeared. I sat there panting, stunned and abandoned. Rosalie had also been mercurial— all Masters were the same.

When would my chance to be mercurial come?

The driver blinked back to life, peering up into the rearview mirror. "Miss—are you okay?"

I hurried belatedly to push down my skirt. "I'm fine. Take me home."

This was Vegas. I knew that he'd seen worse.

CHAPTER THIRTEEN
JACK

As we both walked back from the desert to Sam's convertible I crossed my arms to hold myself, realizing I felt a strange sensation. I was...*cold*. I had been in the cold many times since Rosalie had changed me, but I'd never *felt* cold before. The initial sharp pain of the splash of darkness now radiated out across my entire body, like I had frostbite from it. Whatever it was that'd been trying to take Sam down was chilling.

And hungry.

Like recognized like.

I looked over at Sam, who appeared unwell. "Do you want me to," I began, as we reached her car. She tossed me the keys without question and got into the back seat, laying down. I wasn't sure where to take her to—I sure as hell wasn't going to take her home. Driving back to Dark Ink seemed safest.

I would've raised the convertible's roof, but that would've created more shadows inside the car, something I could now do without. I took off, putting her car through its paces, racing across the night, occasionally looking back in the rear view mirror at her,

74

realizing from the fluttering rise and fall of her chest I was watching her panic.

Whatever it was that'd almost claimed her—it had not been expected.

"Do you do that often?" I twisted to shout back so that she would hear.

"Which part?"

"Talking to dead people."

She sat up at long last, lacing her hands through the front seat headrests. "Not many friends of mine die."

"Lucky you, then," I muttered. "Was that his ghost?" I asked more loudly.

"No. Just an echo of it. His actual soul is safe. Bryan led a clean life," she said. The '*unlike some people*' was implied.

"You knew he was dead. Why did you need to see it?"

"I had my reasons."

"Were they worth risking your life?"

I watched her jaw clench in the rearview. "That doesn't usually happen."

"And what if I hadn't been there?"

She didn't answer me.

I was only now starting to warm up. My brain kept trying to shove the memory of the event back to protect itself, or rush it forward to scare me straight, over and over again. It was like whatever had been attacking her oscillated at the frequency of fear for me, and now I'd be vibrating with it all night.

"You mentioned something about a conduit."

"I don't need to explain myself to you," she said.

"Hey, I don't save people's lives for the hell of it." She pulled back, but didn't let go of the headrests. "Is that—whatever that was —just hanging out on the other side," of what, I had no idea, "or did it come find us? Is it going to be waiting there, if anyone goes back? Did you close off however it got here?"

I knew she heard me. I assumed she was thinking. "Maybe I left myself open a moment too long because I wanted to see him," she confessed. "When you open a door, you can't always be sure what'll come through. Plus—that was a dark place. Your people did bad things there." I watched her chew her lip in reflection. "The ground was used to blood, and now it thirsts."

And who would feed it now? The Sangre Rojo—if Maya sold it to them.

"Can that thing...be turned into a weapon?" I asked.

Her head snapped to look at me—and I realized that if she were truly telekinetic she wouldn't need flying objects to kill me: she could probably twist my head and shoulders in opposite directions.

"Asking for a friend," I clarified.

"Nothing in your dossier says that you'd be interested in that. It's one of the main reasons you're alive now. Do not tempt fate, or me."

"Fair enough." A threat was already an answer. "You have a file on me?"

"Don't let it go to your head. We have files on everyone."

"Who, precisely, is this 'we?'"

She looked at me as though I were insane. "The Faithful. The organization Bryan and I belong to. Rosalie never told you? Did she want you to die?"

"Probably," I answered truthfully. "What does being Faithful even mean?"

"It means that we are unsullied by the outside world, while seeing to the heart of the true inner one. We are bound to serve and protect humanity."

"Even though you're not human?" I looked back at her in the rear view mirror, one eyebrow cocked. I'd seen her levitate things, summon a ghost, and she was fucking gorgeous, in a threatening 'don't touch me, ever' kind of way. Like a tiger up close. Or a hawk.

If Sam wasn't human...what was she?

"Do you always ask so many questions?" she complained.

"Only when I'm driving."

Sam frowned, as I turned down the final road to Dark Ink. "I am human. I'm just pure. My pureness gives me powers."

And now I couldn't help it. I looked fully at her in the rearview, trusting my instincts to handle the road. If pureness meant what I thought it meant....

"Look at me any longer like that and I will separate your eyes from your head."

"Yes ma'am," I said, staring determinedly back at the road.

SOON I STOOD ALONE in Dark Ink's parking lot. From the speed with which she drove away, I had no doubt Sam would not be following me home tonight—although seeing as I had a repetitive schedule, figuring out where I lived probably wouldn't be so hard. One small point in the 'keeping bloodslaves' column—they could protect you from attack during the day. Or, I could just live a clean-ish life, and not require protection.

Good thing the Faithful apparently didn't mind me having sex with a ton of people.

The streetlight made the nearby fence cast shadows, inside Dark Ink was black, and right now even I, a creature of the night, found darkness creepy. Mattie would curse my name when he got here in the morning and I was gone, but hopefully he'd assume the best— that I'd worked hard and taken off early—because I felt I needed to make a pre-dawn stop at Vermillion.

I PARKED the Pack's loaner truck in Vermillion's parking lot. It was decently full, which was bad because anything after four a.m. at a strip club was trouble. If you had better places to be, you'd be there already, drinking hard or getting laid. If you were still at the strip club at 4, chances were you wound up there with no place better to go, so drunk you were hoping beyond hope you'd score a girl—whereas the girls had already scored you. From champagne room solos to fanciful make-out sessions with one another very nearby, dancers were better at creating the illusion of sex at a strip club than Penn and Teller were at anything they did on stage.

I went in, dodged the hostess, and made my way to the back, looking for Maya along the way. A big man—not Tamo big, but respectable—tried to turn me around. The temptation to show him who was boss loomed large, but now that I knew I had my own Faithful Santa judging whether I was naughty or nice, I just told him to tell Maya I was here with a whammy.

Five minutes later, Maya emerged. From her expression I was clearly unexpected and unwelcome, but she gestured me back nonetheless.

"It's tomorrow night at midnight, Jack," she reminded me, heaving a sigh as she led me back through the public dressing room.

"I haven't forgotten."

"Then why are you here?" She was worried I wanted to renegotiate our deal. Of course. It's what she would've done. One of her hands pressed open the door to Rosalie's old dressing room which was apparently where I'd interrupted her as there were two women and one man hog-tied on the ground.

"Hors d'oeuvre?" she asked. The man's eyes were wide open in terror.

I made a show of nudging him with my shoe. "Depends. Are they caged or free range?"

"Duck-duck-goose," she said, pointing out the two women first who were smiling. They, no doubt, had been responsible for the goose's capture. "Don't worry, Jack. We'll have our fun with him and then we'll set him free. Anemia can feel a lot like a really bad hangover—he need never know."

"I actually have business to discuss."

Maya pouted at me and put her hands on her hips. "Do you really, or are you just saying that to make my life difficult?"

"I'm here, aren't I?" I held my arms wide. This was where Rosalie had turned me—and where I'd slept with Maya after being turned, not knowing any better. I had no love for Vermillion in general and this room in particular.

She made a disgusted sound and yanked on one of the girl's quick-ties, releasing her wrists, then leaned over looking at the man. *"Everything after your second drink is a blur now. You don't remember anything that happened—other than having a fantastic time. One girl even gave you a blow job."*

"We don't have to, do we?" the rising girl asked, setting the other girl's wrists free, before working on her ankles.

"I just might, for fun," the other said.

"Go-go-go," Maya said, shooing them along. Between the two of them, they carried the now semi-comatose man out. Maya turned toward me. "I hope whatever you're going to tell me will be worth it."

"Yeah—I'm thinking you need to cancel that appointment with the Rojo tomorrow night."

Her eyes narrowed. "Why?"

"Because there's something bad out there." I told her about the evening I'd had with Sam, as she looked increasingly pained.

"You talked to a Faithful?"

"Yeah."

"You've got the luck of an idiot, Jack. You do realize that they kill us, with very little provocation?"

"I'm beginning to get that picture, yes."

Maya started pacing. "The Faithful are why Rosalie mostly used humans she controlled. Humans invite less suspicion than vampire armies."

"Look, I really don't care about history—I just don't think you should sell the land. I'm not sure if you'd be giving them a door to another place—or the leash to some kind of hellish monster—but why take the chance?"

She frowned. "Because it's already done."

"But I thought you were leery?"

"My humans got our silver out—and it turns out the land's worth was negligible. The mine was totally tapped decades ago. Its only apparent worth was as a bunker to Rosalie, which your thrilling explosions ruined." She shifted, pushing one shoulder forward. "Plus, they sensed my hesitation and offered double."

I groaned. "If the land's worth nothing to you, why is it worth double to them?"

"I don't care."

"Goddamn it, Maya, not everything's about money."

"Yes, it is, Jack. You may not realize it now, but forever is a long time. And now that your lawyer-friend has gone flitting off to God-knows-where with your werewolf ex-boss, I cannot be sure that Fleur de Lis is going to honor the contract for their club. They haven't even started construction."

I had no doubt Mark had made the contract bulletproof. He was thorough—she was just trying to save face.

"Cancel the sale."

"Why? If whatever it is that's out there is so awful, why would we want to keep it?"

"Because a weapon in the hand is worth more than two in the bush."

"It's impossible. The cash has already been wired. Tomorrow night's merely a formality—the exchange of the deed itself."

I rocked back on my heels. "Just how much do you know about the Rojo anyhow?"

"They're upper-level dealers. They don't run product personally —but they're where the product comes from."

I was going to ask what 'product' was, then decided I didn't want to know. "And why would they want a creepy-ass hungry thing in the ground?"

"I'm unsure."

"Can you stall until we figure it out?"

"Absolutely not." She shook her head, then regained confidence.

"And why would I? They're giving us money, Jack—well, *me*, money. I don't need to care about anything past that."

"How long did Rosalie own that land?" I asked, staring her down.

Maya inhaled to think. "Fifty years. Maybe more."

"Strange how they didn't want to buy it until she'd died."

"Strange how her death coincided with the obliteration of literally anything of worth upon it," she countered.

"Except for whatever it is they're paying you double for. The stunning vistas—of nothing? Or maybe just the cool night air?"

Maya set her shoulders. "I've had enough of suppositions for one night. Can I count on you tomorrow or not?"

I paused. Dark Ink needed me—and so did Paco, who'd be waking up sometime later that night.

"Might I note that if they think we're divided you might meet a bad end—and your tattoo studio could become a money laundering front?"

I'd give even odds on Maya doing that to me, if she thought she could get away with it. "Well when you put it like that," I said. "If only to meet our new monster owning overlords in person."

"And who wouldn't want to?" she asked, sarcastic and gracious both at once. "Tomorrow?"

"Tomorrow. But after that—"

"Nothing to do with me, blah-blah-blah, deal." She waved her hand in the air between us as if slapping.

I'd have had her shake on it, but I knew that promises meant nothing to her. I'd just have to keep setting boundaries for her to merrily skip over, or set on fire and push through. "See you then," I said, and walked off.

I went by Dark Ink and worked the rest of my shift, catching one of Nikki's friends who wanted a cover-up on an arm band he'd gotten done in prison. It required me pounding in a lot of solid black which the guy took like a champ, sitting like a rock even on the soft spots inside near the armpit. I didn't know the name of the gang we were hiding with my flying vampire bat cuff—his choice of artwork, not mine, though we both found it amusing—but it didn't matter. Once you were a member of the Pack, the only way out was to die.

After that, Mattie came in with a lead on two new artists, and wanted to bring them by that day for interviews. I told him that was fine, but that I couldn't be there, prior obligations and all that—with my coffin—but that I trusted his judgment because it was true.

Then I drove home with about twenty minutes to spare. Vegas didn't have huge commuter problems, but with so many tourists renting sports cars and drinking, accidents could easily ruin my morning drive. Today I was lucky and made it home without incident.

Luna had locked the door. I knew I'd find her sleeping on the couch, so I tried to be careful, opening it quietly and pushing it in slowly, which was good because it thudded against her thigh.

She was sleeping on the floor in a tangle of couch cushions and sheets, rather like a dog—and the door nudging her woke her.

"Master," she said, pushing herself up.

"Jack," I corrected her.

She threw her arms around my knees. Her eyes were red with not enough sleep—and possibly crying. "I thought you were dead."

"Why?"

"You went off with a Faithful! How could I not assume the worst?" she said, and started crying again.

"Whoa, whoa, whoa." I walked forward, pushing her back so that I could close the door. "I survived. Why didn't you sleep on the couch?"

She didn't answer me, she just kept sobbing. I hovered over her, unsure what to do next, with the lingering feeling that I was still getting played—until she hiccupped, and kept cry-hiccupping, becoming even more pathetic.

Up until now, the saucy, sexy, insane girl I knew seemed to have had standards, whereas the woman currently clinging to my legs was a mess. I sighed—I only had fifteen minutes left. I leaned over and scooped her up and everything she was surrounded with, carrying her easily to the couch, where I carefully dropped her down. I expected her to hold on, to use our proximity as an excuse for closeness, but once on the couch she turned away.

"I'm sorry for scaring you," I said.

"Why? It's not like you care. It's not like anyone really does."

"Luna, if you're asking for affection from me—you'd be better off asking Sugar. Or a wall. Go find a real man to love you somewhere."

"I don't want affection," she said, setting up to pat the couch cushions roughly back into shape. "I just want to be somebody's slave. And have that person actually deserve me. For them to use me. Like I was meant to be used. It's what I'm good at." She was punching pillows in lieu of punching me.

"That's not ever going to be me, either."

"Why? Because of your stupid pride? Stupid pride's going to get you killed, Jack." I glared at her, as she went on. "Don't look at me like that—not by me. By someone like that girl you ran off with, without thinking, without backup."

I shook my head. "Well, you may have a point there. But that burden is mine alone."

"Who else is going to turn me if you die?"

I squatted on my heels so our heads were even. "Who else is going to turn you now? Because it won't be me."

She dragged the sheets up to her chest, fat tears leaking down her cheeks. "I did everything for Rosalie. And you—just Dark Ink— just a secretary?" she sputtered.

"I'm sorry I don't know anyone for you to kill. Maybe you can patch things up with Maya."

The glare she gave me let me know what she thought about that.

"I saw her tonight. She's not always evil."

"She's not evil enough," Luna complained. "She thinks she's smarter than she is. She'll get in over her head someday."

On that, we agreed. "What do you know about the Sangre Rojo?"

She swiped the sheet across her eyes and shook her head. "Bad news. Rosalie wouldn't deal with them. Said they were too dangerous—too violent. And for Rosalie, that was saying something." Luna blotted her nose with the back of her hand. "And they've got a weird caste system. All their vampires are men. All their bloodslaves are women. Very pretty girls though. I met one, once."

I rocked back to standing. "Good to know. Thank you."

"You're welcome."

She gave me a look both hopeless and helpless, the look of a castaway seeing a ship pass by too far to be seen, and in that moment I was tempted, truly tempted, to turn her, just because she desired it so much.

But first, I needed to go back and lay down with the person I'd already turned. One experiment at a time.

It wasn't until I was laying against Paco's back that I realized I'd never told her Samantha was a Faithful—and that the weapon she had was clearly meant to be used against one.

Then the dawn claimed me.

CHAPTER FOURTEEN
LUNA

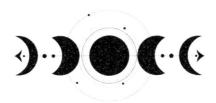

Had I done it? I chewed on the inside of my lip, lying on the couch. I'd never tried being honest *and* scared before. I'd spent the intervening hours after seeing my new Master at Jack's, working myself up into a state with memories of my mother and the future that would claim me if I couldn't get a vampire to change me. It'd been embarrassingly easy to really cry.

But it'd been worth it! The look he'd given me at the end, before the dawn had come—he'd been thinking about biting me—and more.

If Jack turned me first, would I still need my strange other Master? Which one would I rather be linked to for eternity? My current Master would have more power, clearly—but Jack would be less bossy. Both of them were likely equally neglectful.

I flatted the sheets out over myself. Between Jack shoving me away and my other Master's sudden abandonment in the car—while it wasn't unusual to feel disregarded...it hurt more now. Especially when I'd been so close to always mattering, to earning my own slaves which I could then ignore in turn. I was sniffling ruefully, still feeling sorry for myself, when I heard a tap at the door.

Girl Scouts or solicitors. Goddammit.

I swept the sheets off and went to the door, opening it without looking through first—whoever was on the other side deserved the version of me they were going to get.

I found Zach there—that blond boy from the other morning. I knew his name from hearing Jack call it out several times.

"Hey," he said, clearly surprised I'd answered.

"Hey yourself," I said. "Jack's not here right now."

He took me in. I looked like I'd just rolled out of bed and possibly onto another bed made of nails, and then rolled off that one too. "Are you okay?"

"It's been a long night. Can I take a message? I'd like to get back to sleep."

He glanced behind me, to where my bed on Jack's couch was clear. "Uh, sure. Just—tell Jack I came by?"

"Sure."

He nodded then stepped back—then inhaled as I began to shut the door. "Actually—don't tell him I was here? I shouldn't have come by."

I snorted. "I know how that feels. I'll give him whatever message you want."

"Thanks," Zach said, dropping his shoulders and clearly feeling sheepish.

"Don't worry about it. We should form a support group or something." Even if Zach wasn't a true bloodslave, Jack cared for him—which made him possibly useful for me.

Zach laughed. "Probably. I'm in apartment twenty-one. And my name is Zach."

"I'm Luna," I said, smiling at him before closing the door.

CHAPTER FIFTEEN
JACK

I woke alone in a pit, surrounded by darkness personified, with nothing around for as far as I could sense or see—just coldness. Omnipresent coldness. Chilled to the bone. The cold of the grave.

And then I really woke up, gasping for air, arms wrapped around Paco.

I blinked, trying to regain my equilibrium. I couldn't remember the last dream I'd had—it had to have been before I was turned—but now I knew that vampires could have nightmares.

Up until last night, the worst thing in my life had been being involved in a cave-in, trapped underground, worried that I would live forever and no one would ever free me. Now—I sat up in bed, still panting—it was just cold nothingness. Like space, but without stars, for eternity. I shuddered and then lay back down.

Paco was going to wake up tonight, after three in the morning. I nestled against him, taking comfort in his familiar form, his familiar scent. What was he going to think when he woke up? And how was I going to feed him? Sex with me wouldn't be enough anymore— vampires were takers of life, not givers, a human partner would be far more satisfactory.

Would he want to go back to his boyfriend? What would his boyfriend think, after he was gone all this time? What would've happened at his job? I brushed a hand through his hair. I didn't mean to make a mess of things for him. I just couldn't let him die. I hoped he understood that. I hoped I'd made the right choice.

I kissed the nape of his neck again, and this time really got out of bed. Sugar wasn't there waiting for me—I went into the living room to find that Luna had already fed her, whenever it was that she'd gotten up. The couch cushions were neatly replaced and the sheets folded. I wondered if tomorrow it would be Paco sleeping on the couch—or in my bed.

Hopeful—and nervous—I got in the shower.

I was at Dark Ink to touch base an hour later. Luna was behind the counter again. After our talk this morning, I didn't know which version of her I'd find, she was all over the map—but this time when she saw me she squealed my name and ran to my side.

I hugged her because she was hugging me so I couldn't not with everyone watching, and yet—she looked up at me and gave me a mischievous wink, knowing I was trapped.

Past her though, things looked full—the station opposite mine had a man I didn't recognize working behind its partition. When he saw me, he apologized to his client and stood up to come over. He was taller than I was and had tan skin, with a strong brow and a short round beard. When he reached me he took off his gloves and offered his hand.

"I'm Nilesh. Mattie told me you'd be coming in." He had a slight Indian accent.

"I'm Jack—nice to meet you."

"Mattie hired him this morning, apparently," Luna chimed in. "His paperwork's on your desk, and I've added his work to all the portfolios, including online."

"Thanks, Luna," I told her. I didn't even know how to add things to our webpage—I turned to him. "What's your specialty?"

"American traditional."

"Always a popular choice. How do you know Mattie?"

"Friend of a friend, from the convention circuit. I'm looking to have a home shop here while I go out on the weekends."

Weekends were our busiest times, but beggars for warm and talented bodies could not be choosy. "Sounds good."

"I worked his calendar out already, boss," Luna said, her tone sexy, the word 'boss' a tease. I glared at her, but she was grinning, and I had a feeling I'd be boss-this and boss-that all night. I sighed.

"Hey man," Nilesh went on. "I've seen your stuff before, it's tight —how come you don't tour?"

Luna wrapped her arm through mine. "Jack's a homebody is why."

Then the door chime behind us rang and Luna freed herself to go say hi, the embodiment of the perfect employee once again. It was like this morning had never happened. The girl gave me whiplash.

"If I had her to come home to, I would tour less too," Nilesh confessed, his voice low.

"Believe it or not—she makes me want to go on tour," I said. "Like a long one. Around the world." Nilesh's bushy eyebrows rose and he laughed.

As did his client behind him. I hadn't really looked hard earlier, trying to grant them whatever privacy the partition afforded, but now I did as his client leaned up and back, stretching up from their chair like a cat.

"Sam?" I said in surprise. From as close as I was, I could see she was naked from the waist up. Her breasts were perfect, high on her chest, her areolas wide and dark, and the sight of her made the hunger lurch inside of me, like a pit bull pulling on a chain, reminding me I hadn't fed it last night.

"Just getting a touch-up," she said. Nilesh returned to her side, and she bent back down.

Luna returned after setting up a walk-in with a portfolio. "I told her she couldn't just wait for you—she had to spend some money."

I chastised Luna. "She could've just waited."

"No, the timing was good," Sam said, from behind the shoji-screen wall. "Gimmie fifteen minutes, will you?"

"Sure." I had a feeling she was here for a reason, it wasn't just a social call. But her timing was bad—I had a lot on my plate this evening. I needed to feed, I needed to back-up Maya, and then I needed to get home before Paco woke, and then with him figure out how best to feed him. I'd texted Francesca, one of my local hook-ups for blood, but she hadn't texted me back yet. Luna was watching me, and she'd been around Rosalie too long not to know what I was thinking.

"I am literally right here," she said, swiveling her head to show me both sides of her neck.

"Yes you are, and yet, no," I answered her, ducking into my office as Nilesh finished up.

Sam met me there. I gave her the office chair and stood to lean against the desk. I was curious about what Nilesh had done to her, but I didn't want to ask her to move her bandage—she was far too attractive to be alone with half-naked.

"Just because I'm pure doesn't mean I'm a prude," she said with a smirk.

Somehow all the women I knew could read my mind. "So what's up?"

"I talked to my superiors. We'd like your help to quarantine that land."

"Your people want my help?" I tilted my head. "Why?"

"They don't believe I made an error. Nothing followed Bryan through the conduit—I tapped into something that was already out there. Until we know what that was, we need to make sure no one else gets hurt."

"Small problem. That land isn't mine. And the woman it belongs to just sold it. The transaction will be finalized tonight."

Sam's teeth ground together. "Who will own it next?"

"The Sangre Rojo."

She rocked back and the back of the chair hit her fresh tattoo, making her hiss. "Shit, shit, shit."

"I thought pure people didn't curse?"

"I'm pure of heart, not pure of tongue." She stood, looking for somewhere to pace.

"I take it you can't arrange a quarantine with them."

"Let's just say the Faithful and the Rojo are not on speaking terms. Have your friend, the current owner, call off the deal."

"Already tried that, last night. She likes money more than she likes helping people. It's a bad trait among my kind. Plus, she's afraid of pulling out on them." I watched her grimace. "From your reaction, sounds like she has reason to be."

"The Rojo are irrational. They pursue dark magic and follow dark gods. Whatever their interest in that land is, it cannot be good. They likely know more than we do already."

"Literal gods? Like—you people know about an afterlife?"

"Gods like semi-physical manifestations of the will of groups of beings combining psychic power towards one purpose." She took in the confused look on my face and simplified for me. "Like a religion —only one where prayers work and you use them to kill things."

"That sounds bad."

"Because it is."

Sam wasn't the only one with the urge to pace. I needed to figure out how I was going to get Maya out of this mess—I didn't want Dark Ink to sink with her. "I don't suppose you want to join forces for the night?"

Sam stood up straighter. "How so?"

"Maya, kin to me through Rosalie, is meeting the Rojo at Vermillion at midnight tonight to hand over the deed. I was going to go and help her make a show of force. I don't think she can back out of the deal without dying—or without help. But if all the Rojo that show up mysteriously wind up dead, then, well, we outnumbered them."

"You would only be making yourselves targets."

"Ahh, but you'll arrive to help us kill them all. If we blame you and claim casualties as well, then their anger would be misplaced. You'll have the deed and we'll repay the Rojo, there won't be any witnesses, and maybe we all survive."

One of her eyebrows arched. "That is a wildly improbable plan."

"Agreed. But do you have a better one?" I nudged the mouse, turning on the computer screen behind me to check the time. "Because you've got about three hours till midnight."

Sam frowned deeply, furrowing her forehead. "I'll have to communicate with my superiors."

"All right," I said, moving for the door. She blocked it with her body and held her hand up for silence, while closing her eyes.

"Okay," she said, after a long pause. "They're in agreement."

I inhaled to ask how she knew, but then realized telepathy was only a skip, hop, and a jump away from telekinesis. Being a Faithful seemed a lot like being the protagonist in an '80s Stephen King novel.

"What about you and yours?" she asked.

"Maya won't be happy but she'll listen to common sense. I'll make her. How many reinforcements will you be bringing?"

Sam flashed me a wolfish grin. I had a feeling she enjoyed fights. "Enough of them. What time should we arrive?"

I imagined there would be a period of metaphorical dick-waving before business commenced—but I also knew vampire conversations could get deadly, fast. "Ten after. Fifteen at the latest. And remember—not a single Rojo can survive."

Sam grunted. "And just like that, you're willing to condemn so many that you've never met." She made it sound like we weren't in agreement—like it was a character flaw.

"If it means that that thing in the desert that's a portal to a cold dark hell doesn't open again, yes." I leaned past her and opened up the door behind her. Luna was hovering nervously right outside, as was Nilesh, presumably looking to get paid. I jerked my chin at Luna.

"Pay and tip him from the register. Her tattoo is on the house."

Nilesh's eyes widened as Sam strode out. "See you soon, Jack. Between now and then, stay good."

"We both know that's doubtful," I said, then she was gone.

CHAPTER SIXTEEN
JACK

Luna generously paid out Nilesh and then ran to my side. "You absolutely, positively, cannot trust her." Behind her, Nilesh started packing up his kit. It was already nine. The place had thinned a little while I was in the office, but that was normal for a weeknight near the end of the month. People were always more interested in covering rent than in getting tattoos.

I looked to Luna. "Someone told me that about you, and you're still here."

She put her hands to her temple as though holding back a headache. "Yes, but they were wrong. I'm not. Have you asked yourself what she is getting out of it, at least?" She was speaking in a rough whisper—but other people were still watching.

"This is not the time nor the place, Luna. We'll talk about it later."

"When?"

"My place. Eleven. Be there."

"Why? Where are you going?"

"Out to get dinner." She knew what I meant—someone else's blood that wasn't hers.

Luna's eyes narrowed and I knew she wanted to shout at me. Instead, her hands clenched into fists and her whole body shook with barely contained anger. "Fine," she said, and turned on her heel, stomping away.

I almost felt bad pissing her off, except that now it'd become sort of a pattern. Plus she was right the other morning—I was bad enough with Zach. I didn't need another human I could take for granted long term, look where that'd gotten me with Paco.

All I needed right now was a human I could take for granted for an hour.

I hopped into my car and drove to the Strip.

I'D HAVE to get Luna to find Betty tomorrow. I'd left her—my beautiful 1963 Lincoln Continental—outside of Mark-the-lawyer's house, and she'd probably been towed by now. The loaner truck the Pack had given me probably needed to be returned, and it wasn't exactly a girl-or-guy magnet-type. I couldn't tell you what kind of truck it was and I was driving it, it was that bland.

So I parked a little off the Strip in a hotel lot and caught a cab to the Fleur de Lis so no one would know. There was an upscale club there that I might barely get into dressed like I was, because it was early in the night and I knew how to tip bouncers, but not if anyone saw me getting out of the Pack's ride.

I could've gone to any of the numerous 'dive bars' in Vegas, the ones you see on the TV shows that purport to capture our great town —or any of the actual dive bars that didn't make the cut, the ones in strip malls, with the faded yellow signs. But I'd learned that even in dive bars people took their sweet time to get drunk. No one was looking for adventure at a dive bar. Dive bars didn't show up as background sets on glamorous reality shows where people got swept off their feet. No one wanted to sleep with anyone from the cast of *Cheers*, not really—and in gay clubs, things didn't even get started until at least eleven. I needed to be home by then—so I was taking my chances at the Fleur de Lis's club.

The elevator doors opened. The hostess wasn't even at her station—I just walked on in and started being me.

If I wanted to, I could exude a kind of vampiric charisma. Mind you I'd gotten plenty of play as a human, but being a vampire was something more. Often as not, people would come over to me, men and women, and just start talking. Sometimes so much so it was hard to get them to stop—I'd had plenty of conversations I'd had to whammy my way out of for sanity's sake.

When I had the time, it was nice. It was good to remember what being human was like. And I wasn't particularly picky about who I slept with. I viewed it as my personal mission to give as many people as possible a very good time. They took home Vegas stories and I went home sated, it was a win-win.

But I couldn't leave tonight to chance. I only had ninety minutes, and I was ethically averse to whammying people into sex with me. So I'd have to pick my prey carefully and then very quickly show them a fabulous time.

I walked up to the bar and ordered a Manhattan, taking a quick glance up and down to see who else's drink was getting low. A man across the bar was also looking at me. Our eyes met and held. He was positively Nordic, both in appearance and stature, and I felt the hunger writhe inside me in anticipation. Men were so much easier than women—

"Order me one too?" said a woman's voice beside me.

I broke eye-contact with him to look at her. She was mind-numbingly gorgeous. Possibly professionally so. I didn't mind paying for sex occasionally, but I had a feeling I couldn't afford her.

"Sure," I said, jerking my chin at the bartender who'd overheard.

"Thanks," she said, giving me a subtle smile. She had waves of dark hair, pinned back by a real rose—I could smell it. Her body was perfectly proportioned; curves, breast, waist, hips, swooping in and out, wearing a green satin dress with a halter top, and in perfectly matching green sandals that tied around the ankle. Her skin was light brown, her eyes were darker, and her lips were full and painted a perfect red, and somehow she was alone.

That was the professional kicker. No girl who looked like her ever needed to be.

The bartender returned with her cocktail and she raised it to her lips, taking a sip and closing her eyes to savor it before saying, "Thank you."

"You're welcome...?"

"Camila," she said, with a light accent.

"Jack." I tilted my glass to hers to make them clink. "Come here often?" It was a bad line, but it worked.

She laughed. "No. Just tonight. Drove up from L.A. Needed to get my head on straight."

"Why? If you don't mind me asking." I already knew she'd tell me. My charisma was at work.

"I thought I was going to get a part, but I didn't. It went to some other girl instead."

"In a movie?" I guessed.

"No. In a car commercial." She pouted preemptively. "Don't laugh."

"I wouldn't dare," I said, sincerely.

Her full lips curved up into a smile. "I'm a good actress, you know? But it's so hard to get ahead there. And no matter what they say about open calls—they mostly want you blonde. And skinny."

I gave her an appreciative scan. "That may be what they want, but much of the rest of the world disagrees."

"If only L.A. were in Nicaragua then. I would be so marketable!" She laughed, and took another sip of her drink. "Anyhow. I've taken up enough of your time. Thanks for the drink."

"It was my pleasure," I said. I wanted to keep her there, but the Nordic man was more of a sure thing and time was of the essence. She lifted her glass in salute and sashayed away, giving her phone a glance. I couldn't help but watch her go.

Just as I was about to turn back to the bar, she turned as well and trotted back up to me. "What about you?" she asked.

"What about me?"

"Do you disagree?" She gave me a look that was challenging yet hopeful. "With that casting director?"

Whatever-the-fuck-did they put in the water in LA, to make a woman who looked like her insecure? "He made the biggest mistake of his life," I told her, sincerely.

She gave a slight gasp, and then seemed to come to a decision, setting her drink down on the bar before grabbing my wrist. I set my drink down it and let her pull me.

We were in the elevator before she spoke again—and she had a room key. She swung it over the keypad and pressed a number. "You won't judge me, will you?" she asked.

"Never," I swore.

"I have a side-piece up here. He keeps me afloat. I can't waitress all the time, or I'd never have time to audition." She spoke in a rush, as if trying to convince me.

"That makes sense," I assured her.

"We were supposed to meet at the bar, but his flight was delayed —he won't be in for another few hours. So...." The elevator doors opened, and she leaned up to kiss me.

Camila's lips were as sweet as I had hoped, and they parted for me, letting me gently push my tongue in. She folded into me as I wrapped my arms around her, keeping my hands chastely on her waist. The satin was smooth and enticing, practically asking them to roam. As the doors were about to close again, I swung an arm out to stop them and pulled my head back. "Is this your floor?"

Her eyes were wide and she nodded, breathily saying, "Yes."

Camila's hand found my wrist again and pulled me down the hallway, looking this way and that, worried about getting caught. I didn't know about her, but that made it hotter for me—that and listening to her breathe roughly as we walked below a jog, me watching the way her ass wriggled in that skirt—and how I could now see that she had on stockings with Cuban seams. When we got to her room at the end of the hall, she swiped the key.

"Can I come in?" I asked her, once she was on the other side. The key made it a private residence—by vampire rules I had to ask.

"Of course you can," she said, and pulled back.

The room was palatial—less a room and more a residence—and on a table in the center of it was a bouquet of roses, where the one in her hair had come from, no doubt.

When the door was closed, she turned toward me and leaned against it, flush with the excitement of what we were about to do. "His wife is a blonde. So even though I'm the one he wants, I'm not the one who gets to live like this."

I hated him on principle. "Then you should leave him."

Camila looked taken back, and then shook her head with a short laugh. "I will. Someday. But not tonight." She brought a knee up so her foot stamped against the closed door behind her, her satin skirt rising at a precipitous rate. "I only have an hour. Hurry?" she asked me—and so I did.

CHAPTER SEVENTEEN
JACK

I stepped in to kiss her again, pressing her against the door, and this time I let my hands search her body, feeling the satin stretched over her hips and down her thighs. I reached for its edges, kissing her hard as I hauled her skirt up, and found her stockings clipped to garters, with no underwear beneath, just a strip of finely trimmed dark hair—discovering that made it feel like I was opening up someone else's present.

I pulled back, licked my fingers, and reached down to circle her clit and tease at the edges of her pussy, feeling it part for me as she moaned, rolling her head back as I fingered her. I started kissing her neck and asking questions. "Here? The table? The bed?"

"Not the bed. The bed he'll know," she gasped out as I dipped two fingers inside her.

"The table it is then," I said. I pulled my fingers out of her slowly —and then picked her up by her waist, carrying her and spinning us until her ass was against its cool marble top. She gasped as it touched her skin, then reached behind herself to untie and unzip her top, making its green satin spill across her thighs. I pushed her knees wide. This table was the perfect height. I rocked my hips in towards hers—and then sank down.

I needed to be fed—I needed to be *sure* I would be fed—and there was no way more certain than eating a woman out. I spread her wide with my hands and started kissing her where the trail of fur ended.

"Oh fuck," she whispered, rocking back on the table, twining one hand in my hair. She set her gartered thighs on my shoulders and locked her ankles against my back, surrounding me with her. I purred, and guarding my teeth with my lips, took her clit in, sucking at it like I was pulling the juice from a peach.

She made a high pitched whine at that and her hips started to squirm as her ass clenched and pulsed, rocking herself against my mouth. I kept rolling my tongue against her clit, grinding my chin in, pulling her labia wide so she'd feel full even though she wasn't. Behind me, her calves clenched and her feet kicked, and I knew I had found her spot, I could feel the sensations race through her every time my tongue pressed her there, and she started just to curse, "Fuck, fuck, fuck, fuck," like it was an incantation, urging me on. She was so close there was no way I would stop now, even if her man walked in, I would just whammy him into silent forgiveness. I was eating her out like my life depended on it, because in some small way it did—her voice rose, the hand in my hair tightened, and her legs went tense and still, and then her body thrashed against the marble as she shouted, her ass bucking her hips into my mouth as she cried out, again and again.

The life from her orgasm washed out of her in a wave that splashed through me. I followed all her writhing with my mouth and tongue, trying to drink up every drop, as she fell into spasmodic shudders.

"Oh," she said, finally relaxing, sliding her legs off of my shoulders like she was dismounting a horse. "Oh my," she breathed again, barely sitting up.

"Was that what you needed?" I asked her, kissing the inside of her thigh. Her breasts were visible now, and I hadn't even gotten to touch or kiss them. There was so much of her body left to explore.

"Yes," she breathed, looking down at me, her eyes glazed with pleasure.

Technically, I'd had enough—I could make it through the night easy, at least until I went hunting later with Paco—but looking up at her I couldn't help myself. I kissed her thigh again and asked, "Do you want more?"

She silently nodded.

"Good. Because God—I want to be inside you," I said, rising to a stand. I undid my belt and pushed down enough of my jeans to free myself, pulling on a condom quickly. "You're not the only one who has someplace else to be tonight. So I'm sorry if this is fast—"

"Shut up and fuck me," she commanded.

I grinned at her, then grabbed her hips and slid her over to me, reaching between us to tilt myself down, thrusting into her hard.

I knew she was wet enough to take me, but her tightness came as a surprise to us both. She moaned, letting her jaw drop further as I pulled her hips forward, sealing myself inside of her. "Oh God, yes, please," she said, and I started to stroke.

She wrapped her arms around my neck to hold on as I thrust and rocked her back and forward, feeling my cock plunge in and out of her. She made high sounds with every stroke, and her body ground against mine, her stockinged legs winding around me once again, her breasts bobbing in perfect time. I kissed her savagely, her neck, her ears, her throat, finally tasting those breasts as I leaned her down, sucking and pinching her nipples hard, and the rose fell from her hair, giving up.

I felt her hips wind and tense, and she rocked back, holding herself up now with her arms from behind, casting her head back, the bouquet of roses behind her looking like the halo of a radiant saint.

"Oh Jack, fuck me, fuck me," she pleaded as her hips pulsed. I growled, and lowered my whole body over hers until she collapsed and I could reach the table's far side, making her take every inch of me, the vase over our heads teetering with each thrust. She gasped deeply, and then her lips opened in a silent scream as she came for me a second time, her body wracked by rough waves as her nails clawed my back.

I paused for a moment, letting myself absorb her life, feeling it fill me—and then I was pounding her again, claiming her, taking her like she was mine. I finished inside her, coming hard with a guttural growl until all my heat spilled out.

I held myself up over her, breathing hard, as she swept locks of sweaty hair away.

"That was good," she whispered, like her man could be coming down the hall.

"It was," I agreed, daring one last kiss. Then I pulled out and went to the bathroom to flush away the condom—and by the time I got back, she was naked, except for her garter belt, stockings, and a cell phone.

"His flight won't be here till morning time now. Stay with me?"

This was the hazard of giving humans what they wanted. "Camila," I warned.

She turned and yanked out one of the roses from the vase to hand to me. "Come on. It's like one of those bachelor shows. I choose you. Spend the night?" She smiled winningly at me. "We can even get room service on his tab. Caviar? Definitely wine."

"If I could, I would, believe me," I said, taking the rose from her hand, because she offered it.

She gasped as I did so—the florist had missed clipping a thorn, and there was a bright red drop on her thumb. She held it out to me with a pout, and for a moment the world narrowed to just that one drop of delicious blood, reminding me what I had to do and why I couldn't stay.

"I'm sorry. I can't," I said, stepping back and shaking my head.

Her pout intensified. "You're not leaving me for a blonde, are you?"

"Not hardly."

She was a little shorter now without the heels, but still divine, and I wanted to ask for her number, but my policy was generally to let the girl ask me. I didn't need to chase people who didn't want me —and I didn't need to give random humans trouble. "This was," I began, looking around for a gentle escape.

"The best sex of your life," she finished for me, and then walked over to the door. She opened it up for me with her good hand, sucking the blood off of the other's thumb, as she stood behind it, proudly naked.

I was never going to see her again. She didn't need to know how much competition she had—or how long my life would be. "Definitely," I agreed. "I'll keep an eye out for you in the movies," I said, as I stepped into the hall.

"You'd better." And because she knew the coast behind me was clear, she stood in front of the open door, daring me to resist her. Between her youth and beauty and attitude—and the twin scents of sex and blood—it was almost, but not quite, impossible.

"Good-bye, Camila," I said, nodding, and then turned and walked away, determined not to look back.

Whoever her lover was—he had his hands full.

CHAPTER EIGHTEEN
LUNA

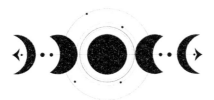

I was outside Jack's apartment at ten-forty-five, keys in hand. I was pretty sure I'd beaten Jack back here—I put my ear to the door and didn't hear anyone moving around inside.

Which didn't entirely prove that Paco wasn't just inside the door, awake and waiting to be fed. I decided to wait—and ten minutes later, Jack showed up, smelling like sex.

"You smell like girl," I complained, as he pulled out his keys.

"Occupational hazard," he said, unlocking the door for the both of us. He held it open for me in a gentlemanly fashion.

"Oh no. You first," I said, sweeping him in with my arms. He gave me a look like I was being ridiculous, but went in, still holding the door so I had to slink by him. I should've used it as an opportunity to grind up, but it was clear someone else had fed him well already. It wasn't just the lingering scent of sex, but the way he held himself. He was positively smug.

Someday, I would get the chance to beat that smugness out of him.

"He wasn't changed until three in the morning, Luna," Jack

explained, taking the lead into the apartment, flipping on lights and kicking off his boots.

"Have you ever seen someone wake up before?" I asked him.

"No."

"Yeah, well," I said, crossing my arms. I hadn't either. But I did know that my predecessor as Rosalie's favorite had been 'accidentally' eaten by Tamo when he'd woken up, and I wasn't going out like that. "I don't know how precise things are. I don't want to take chances."

"About that," Jack said, looking at me. "I need to go talk to Maya tonight."

"And?"

"That's why I asked you to come home. I want you to stay here. Just in case."

My eyes went wide. "No way."

Jack ignored me and fearlessly went back into his bedroom where Paco slept to change his clothes. "I'm not going to miss his waking. It's just that I've got to stop Maya from making a huge mistake."

"Bigger than leaving me here with a fresh vampire?"

"I think so."

I didn't. But I could tell by the way he'd set his shoulders when he emerged that he'd already made up his mind. "What do I do if he wakes up?" I asked.

"He won't. But if he's like me, even though he'll be hungry, he'll wake up sane. The real hunger doesn't hit for an hour or so. So you'll be able to talk him down." He started pulling his boots back on.

"What if he's not like you?" I asked, letting my very real panic tinge my voice. "And remember—he doesn't *know* me."

"At least he knows about vampires though. So he won't require too much explanation—and he'll remember what happened to him, too."

"That he was almost beaten to death by my former Mistress? That's just great." I crossed my arms and held myself while peering into the darkness beyond. "Jack, I thought you were starting to like me."

"I do like you, Luna. I just don't want to like you. Sorry if that doesn't make sense." He stood up after tucking a knife into his boot.

I rocked back and forth, full of indecision. My Master had told me to bind him—what could possibly be more binding than this kind of favor? But what kind of favor could possibly be worse?

"Jack, if I do this, I'm literally risking my life for you—and there's nothing official between us. So what do I get out of the deal? It's all well and good for you to order that boy around, but I know what you can offer—and I know what you're asking of me now."

He hesitated. "All right. If you do this for me—if he wakes, and you shepherd him through it until I get back—then we can talk, all right? Like equals."

Like...equals? Rosalie and I had never had a single conversation like equals. I didn't trust it. "And if he doesn't wake? Doesn't it say a lot about me that you're willing to leave him with me and take that chance?"

Jack considered this, running a hair through his dark hair. "Fair enough. It does. Equal talking, later tonight. No matter what." He stuck out his hand. I took it, and we shook.

"You'd better not be going off to die. Or leaving me here to."

"Neither are in the plans tonight," he said with a cocksure smile, leaving me behind.

JACK LOCKED the door behind him. I waited until surely he was down the hall and unlocked it, worried I might need to bolt.

The door to the bedroom was open, but everything beyond it was dark. I sat on the couch, staring into the darkness like it was a grave.

I had gone and looked, of course.

Years of living under the same roof with Rosalie and I couldn't have told you where she slept during the day if you'd put a gun to my head and a knife to my throat. That was the kind of operation she ran.

But Jack? Just a box. On his bed. To keep the cat out.

He'd tacked up particle board over the room's only window. I hadn't looked on the first day, because it'd just felt too wrong, but by the second I'd wound myself up enough to do it—I ran in, and threw on the light switch, intellectually knowing that he wouldn't know I'd done it, but still afraid of getting caught. After five minutes of not getting busted for that, I'd gone over and pulled the lid of his silly box back, and found both him and his man dead inside.

They were dead-dead. Jack looked asleep, but Paco—well, it was a good thing Jack loved him, right? Because love was blind, and Paco looked worse for the wear. I mean, I'd seen him get beaten—I just sort of assumed becoming a vampire would fix all that. It would, wouldn't it? Or would he have a scar and a puffy eye for life—or his unlife? I guessed I'd find out tonight. Hopefully later—*much later*.

Sugar went in, and I harbored a dark fantasy about using her as the canary in Paco's vampire-coal mine, but she returned with a stuffed mouse and started batting it across the room, blissfully unaware of the danger we were in. She danced with it across the carpeting and then launched it under the couch. I sighed, as she sat back and looked at me expectantly. I looked from the darkness of the bedroom to her and back again. She meowed, knowing she was being ignored.

I didn't hear anything. I didn't see anything. I got off of the couch, knelt beside it, and reached under it to get the mouse out. I grabbed its tail and slung it across the room as I retook my perch on the couch's end, and watched her play with it again.

"I'm jealous of you," I told her.

"Why?" croaked a voice from the bedroom.

I fucking told Jack! I sat on the couch for a long moment, frozen in terror. "Pa-co?" I asked, making his name a question.

"What the hell is this box for?" he asked, his voice thick from disuse.

"That's a long story. Do you...remember what happened to you?"

A pause as dead neurons began firing again. "Yes. Where is Jack?"

"He had something he had to do. He didn't think you'd wake up until later tonight. But I'm his friend, and he left me behind to look after you." I stood, moving incrementally closer to the front door. "Do you know what you are?"

A breathed sigh. "I get the feeling I do, yes. Unfortunately."

It was all I could do not to close my eyes and grind my teeth. I needed to be turned before an illness ruined me—and here I was with another goddamned reluctant vampire.

Everything in the world was unfair.

"Okay, well. You're probably going to be hungry soon. Just please don't kill the messenger, okay?"

There was a rattle from the bedroom as he got out of the box in the dark. "No promises," he said, then after a pause. "That was a joke, by the way."

"Of course it was," I muttered to myself, and then said, "Vampires are known masters of comedy," sarcastically, much more loudly.

He lurched into the hallway. "I feel disgusting. I want to take a shower." He looked better, but sort of scabby—and he saw where I was standing, halfway to the front door. "Are you going to be here when I'm done?"

I swallowed and walked back to the couch to sit down. "As long as you promise not to eat me."

"No promises," he repeated, and shuffled down the hall. "Also, joking."

"Also super funny, ha, ha," I shouted after him. I started pacing as soon as the shower turned on.

TO BE COMPLETELY HONEST, I paced halfway down the hall outside.

I could ditch Paco. He was a grown man, and it wasn't like he could really re-die this evening—he clearly knew the score.

But I wanted my Master to turn me, which meant I needed Jack to owe me—and I actually came up with a plan, so I paced back in time to hear the water turn off.

Paco came out to walk back to Jack's room, wearing a towel. He stopped, seeing me—and I wondered what it was like for him to watch me with a vampire's eyes. Did he...want me? Possibly not, if he was into Jack.

But blood was the great equalizer, and Rosalie had told me more than once that watching mine soar inside me was beautiful.

"My name is Luna," I announced, on the off chance that knowing my name would make him less murdery.

He shook himself, said, "Hey Luna," then went inside the bedroom.

He returned wearing some of Jack's clothing—it was all a little tight on him, because he was more muscular than Jack was, but not tight in a bad way. And the scabs had washed off and the eye had de-puffed—all in all, he was a good looking man, and the way Jack's jeans fit him didn't hurt.

"So—what now?" he asked from the doorway.

I'd checked my phone while he was pulling clothes on. Was Jack done by now? On his way home? He didn't even have my phone number to text me.

"Are you...hungry?" I asked carefully.

His gaze flicked over me. "I could eat."

"About that then," I said. "Let's go."

CHAPTER NINETEEN
JACK

I pulled into Vermillion's parking lot in the truck and found it eerily empty, and when I got out I found a sign blocking the door announcing the club was closed tonight for a private party. The door locked.

I rapped on the glass, and a girl ran up to let me in.

"Hi, Jack," she said, like I ought to know her. I had seen her before once, with Rosalie—when she'd been bringing Rosalie a leash to tie me to a pole.

"Hey," I said, not bothering to ask her her name. "Where's the queen?"

Maya stalked out to the hostess stand. "You're early? On what strange planet?"

"Because we need to talk."

"Again?" She folded her arms. "You're not changing my mind."

"About that," I began, looking around. Our voices echoed without the usually present bass. "I've found a way around the situation."

Her eyes narrowed and she jerked her head sideways. "In the back."

I FOLLOWED her through to the private room where we'd killed Rosalie. It was the first time I'd ever seen it well lit—which explained why humans were milling about, thoroughly cleaning things while wearing club clothes. Near the front dais there were rough hewn tables with empty leather cuffs. A scantily dressed woman with auburn waves was sitting on one of them, and she looked nervous.

"Dare I ask?" I said.

"Treaties are always sealed with blood, Jack. They offer one of their slaves, I offer one of mine, everyone takes a few polite sips, and the deal is done." Maya reached over and ran her hand through the woman's hair. "I wouldn't let anything untoward happen to Zevvi. Not after so recently acquiring her for myself from Rosalie."

No wonder Luna had been so quick to try and find some other owner—although I had no doubt she'd helped Rosalie sign a pact or two while in her service. The woman, Zevvi, swallowed and gave me a brave smile. I fought not to return it—I didn't want to make promises I couldn't keep. I drew Maya into one of the private booths that'd already been cleaned.

"The Faithful reached out to me again. They believe it's imperative that we don't sell that land, Maya. They want us to quarantine it so that all humans stay away."

"It's too late—the wire's gone through."

I eyed her. "You haven't spent the money yet, have you?"

"No."

"Then you'll wire it back."

Maya scoffed dramatically. "I'm not doing something just because the Faithful demand it," she said. "Do you know what kind of precedent that sets? If we work with the Faithful and get caught—other nests will slaughter us as traitors." Bewilderment and disgust fought for control of her expression.

It would have been nice for Sam to mention that, but maybe she assumed I knew I was playing with fire. "So we won't get caught. I came up with a plan B. The Faithful show up here after midnight, help us kill all the Rojo that arrive, and then take the deed themselves. You'll wire the money back, appropriately apologetic, and we'll claim casualties as well. That way we'll have a shared enemy, we won't lose face, and they don't get the land."

"I'll just be out a lot of money, then?" Her tone was sarcastic.

"Cash is replaceable."

"But I'm not!" she hissed. "If your plan blows up, I'll have a target on my back—and you will too! You don't just invite the Faithful into your home, Jack, then offer up other vampires to sate them. What's to say that you're not being played? What's to stop them from killing all of us? And then even if they don't—who's to say they're the best guardians of whatever it was Rosalie left out there?"

"What...she left?" I asked, leaning in. I'd whammy her if I could. "Tell me."

She pulled back. "I don't know. Rosalie had her secrets, all right? And some of them—she kept out there."

"Like what?"

"Like that thing that wanted to eat the boy, remember?"

I recalled the ominous stone coffin that had held something interested in eating Rabbit, Angela's son, so much so that it made the boy turn into a wolf for the first time. "The Sleeper?"

"Yeah—that," she said, with a shudder. "And who knows what else. The mines were bigger than you think, Jack—but then you blew them all up and who the hell cared? I wasn't going to go sifting through the rubble every night." She reached over and clutched my hands, speaking in a terse whisper. "Jack—call them off. The Faithful are just as likely to kill us as they are the Rojo."

I swallowed. I still wanted to believe in Sam—but what was it Luna had told me about my pride and getting myself killed? For the first time since meeting her, I wished I had her and her strange weapon at my side. I opened my mouth, ready to explain that I didn't know how, when one of Maya's people shouted: "Places! They're here! Places!" and it was too late.

Maya growled a curse. "I hope you're happy, Jack. You've killed us both, on the eve of your lover's ascension. I've never met a man with worse timing than you," she whispered, and then stood straight and shouted. "Let them in!"

CHAPTER TWENTY
LUNA

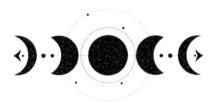

Paco and I stood outside of apartment twenty-one. Paco was looking at me strangely, and I was convincing myself that it had everything to do with the situation and not that he was thirsty for my blood.

"Is Jack here?" Paco asked.

"No—he's busy—we'll see him later, I swear," I said, hurriedly knocking on the door.

"Why are we here then?"

"Play along," I said, knocking some more again.

The door opened, revealing Zach inside. He grinned at me. "Hey —Luna, was it?"

"Hi!" I said, exuberantly. "This is Paco, a friend of Jack's—can we come in?" I hoped me asking on Paco's behalf counted.

"Uh, sure?" Zach said, pulling back. I pushed Paco in ahead of me, in case he needed to re-ask personally, but he easily stepped through the door. Zach's apartment was much the same lay-out as Jack's. "Do you want some water?" he said, gesturing to the kitchen, a little confused.

"No, thank you," I said, arranging myself between him and Paco.

"Look, I know this is weird, but…Jack's a weird guy, right? We can all agree on that?" I nodded strongly, and both of them nodded with me, albeit much more slowly. Zach had no idea where this was going, whereas Paco had begun giving me a look that said he knew exactly where it was going and he didn't like it one bit.

"You may or may not know this, Zach—but Paco's a very, *very* close friend of Jack's. And as such…" I did my best to act coy and bashful, but it was hard. "You both like Jack. So by the theory of sexytimes transference, you should like each other, right?"

And now they were both staring at me. Gawking, really. I had to control the situation, ASAP.

"Zach—you want to be part of the freaky deaky club. I get it," I said with a carefree shrug. "Consider this your invitation. Consider *him* your initiation," I said, with a nod on Paco's side.

Paco gave me a look, condemning this entire idea out of hand, and then sighed. "This is crazy. I'm leaving," he announced. But then Zach moved, and he went still, doing that vampire thing where he was hyper-aware of any motion. I'd seen Rosalie do it a million times.

"It's not," I protested and looked hopefully at Zach. "You want him to love you, don't you?" Zach looked away. "Come on. I was there the other morning. I saw it in your eyes—before you asked Jack out to dinner."

And at that, Paco's stillness became something else—less vampire-frozen and more human-pained, as though hearing a betrayal.

"But he told you he couldn't be in a relationship with you—and this is why," I said, twisting toward Paco. "Paco's the man that Jack loves." Paco's wounded look shifted into a look of warning. "He's the man Jack loves enough to risk everything for."

Paco swallowed, closing his eyes, and I didn't know if he was hoping it was true or if he knew it.

"So why are you here? Why aren't you out with him?" Zach asked the both of us, sounding hurt.

"Because Jack's off on business. And Paco needs something that I can't give him—but it's my duty to take care of him. For Jack. Just—like it's yours."

Zach shook his head while looking at Paco. "That sounds crazy."

"Because it is crazy," Paco apologized. "I'm sorry, I don't know why I listened to her—we never should have come."

We'd followed Zach into his kitchen, so there was a dining chair behind Paco. I pushed him back and he went with it, thudding into its seat. "It is *not* crazy," I said, hovering over him, my hands on the chair's armrests, my breasts and throat near his face—and I saw him tense beneath Jack's too tight shirt, the muscles of his chest rippling. He was aware of me—not as a person, but as a source of energy. His eyes widened, looking up, and I nodded meaningfully. If he was as hungry as I thought he was, he needed to *get with the program*.

"The only thing that is crazy here," I went on, "is that you haven't met yet." I stood up to broadly gesture. "So, Zach—this is Paco, Jack's long-time lover and confidant. Paco—this is Zach, the side-piece Jack doesn't want to admit that he cares for even though he clearly does."

Zach blushed a bit, but was still looking at me like I'd grown a second head.

I waved my hands between them. "Look, I don't have time for honesty. Can we just skip to the kissing?" I tugged my shirt over my shoulders, exposing both my breasts.

"Wait, what?" Zach said, stepping back.

"There's no way I'm going to watch you two fucking and not touch myself. Just because you're gay doesn't mean you have to be cruel."

Paco's head pulled back. "And who said we're going to fuck?" he asked.

"You did. Just there," I said, and started to shimmy my skirt off. This was a management technique Rosalie had taught me more than once—just start demanding people do what you want them to. Like as not, most times it'll happen.

Paco looked over to Zach in disbelief at my actions and Zach gave him a hapless, 'She's clearly insane' look back. Finally something they agreed on.

"Come on, come on. You know you need this," I told Paco, reaching for his shirt, pulling it up his chest, "and you know you want this," I told Zach.

Zach leaned back on the bar behind him. "I'm sorry—I just don't see," he said, but then something clicked. I had Paco's shirt half-way off, exposing his fabulously muscled abdomen and lower torso—which caught Zach's gaze, and then Paco realized Zach was watching. He took his shirt back from me, turning his head and staring at the ground. He was breathing harder—I knew he was tempted, likely more than he'd ever been tempted before in his mortal life. Rosalie had tried to explain the hunger to me more than once before—sometimes she'd used it as a warning and at others an excuse.

But now I could feel the power coalescing in the room. The calm before the storm, as Paco came into himself, his sails unfurling for the first time. I glanced back at Zach, and I could tell that he felt it too.

"How long have you known Jack?" he asked Paco.

Paco let his shirt drop. "Too long," he said, ruefully. "Seven years? Feels like seventy, sometimes." Thanks to Jack turning him, that could actually be a reality, if they both still liked each other's company and managed to survive. "You?" Paco asked back.

"Less than a month," Zach said, a little sheepish.

Paco gave him a sly grin, mimicking one of Jack's looks almost perfectly. "Don't be embarrassed. He has that effect on people. He doesn't even know he does it, half the time."

Zach held his stomach as if punched. "That almost makes me feel worse."

"It wasn't meant to. The first time you sleep with him, well, what can I say—our boy's easy." Paco shrugged. "But if you're past that though, to a third or more—well—you're in far more rarified company."

"Like yours?" Zach asked, risking giving him a grin back.

"Precisely."

I pinched the bridge of my nose. I had never been this naked *and* ignored. They were talking like they were alone on some kind of blind date. "Skip to the kissing," I said. "Or straight to the fucking, I don't care—just move it along." I didn't want to mash them together like Barbie dolls, but no matter what it was that Paco thought, how well he believed he could control himself, we did not have all night.

"Why? You want to watch?" Paco asked, standing up again, coming near. I could feel the electricity around him—he was like a walking storm. I swayed, wanting to follow him, to serve him, even though I knew better.

"As I previously said, yes. I'm a good watcher," I said, glancing at Zach. "Ask him. He knows." Zach flushed red beneath the remnants of his tan. "The other morning I wasn't supposed to look, but I couldn't help myself. I watched him and Jack give each other blow jobs."

"You did, did you?" Paco asked Zach, who quietly nodded, eyes wide. "I was Jack's first. I taught him everything he knows."

Zach laughed nervously. "Then—thank you—because that man," Zach said, as Paco leaned in, blocking his next words with a kiss.

I stood stock still, waiting to see how Zach would react. He tensed for a moment—and then melted into Paco's waiting arms. Paco leaned Zach back against the bar, pressing bodily up against him, and I knew that he was hard—and wanted Zach to know it. I was worried, for Zach's sake again—until his hands started greedily pulling up the back of Paco's t-shirt.

Everything unfolded in front of me like the world's most perfect porno. I mean, I'd seen sex before, and had had a lot of it—but this was like an intimate performance, almost one on one, except for the fact that I wasn't personally involved. Paco's hands found Zach's belt and started undoing the buckle—I heard the jingle as metal hit metal once it was free—and then saw Paco pull Zach toward him, before roughly shoving Zach's pants down, revealing Zach's heavy cock.

Paco pulled back and Zach swooned, breathing heavy. Paco yanked Zach's shirt up and started kissing down, as Zach wound one of his hands through Paco's hair and whispered, "If you're anything like him then—oh God," to himself, just as Paco's mouth found him hard.

Paco moved to kneel before the blond, stroking one hand up the plane of Zach's flat stomach and wrapping the other around Zach's thigh to grab his ass. Zach moaned, throwing his head back, clutching the bar with his free hand like he was trying to hold on. "Oh God," he whispered, as if to himself, as his hips started to pulse in Paco's time. "Oh God, oh God."

Paco made a pleasured sound, drawing Zach's cock out of his mouth until just the head bobbed inside, making a show of sucking it, before taking his shaft in his hand. "There's nothing Jack's done to you that I didn't do to him, first," he said, licking up the bottom of Zach's shaft, before kissing the head of his cock again.

Zach curled forward and put both his hands on Paco's shoulders, jaw dropped. "Don't torture me, like he does—I can't take that right now."

A wicked smile played over Paco's lips. "Not today then," he promised, and went back down.

I honestly forgot to touch myself. I had every intention of doing it earlier—the more we fed Paco, the safer we were—and I did feel like a bit of an asshole for helping to put Zach's cock into a hungry vampire's mouth without warning him. But as they went on, I just took it all in: how Paco stroked Zach's cock while he licked and sucked his balls, the way Zach's body writhed, letting you know instantly how much you were pleasuring him, the soft sucking sounds of Paco's mouth as he worked Zach, Zach's perfect groans in response—I was sitting quietly in the chair Paco had vacated, transfixed.

And then Zach grabbed his hands around Paco's head and his

hips started bucking just as he began shouting. I heard Paco growl encouragement as Zach thrust forward and surely lost himself inside Paco's mouth.

Zach twitched with full body shudders after that, as Paco sucked the rest of his cum out of him—then seemed to come to his senses again, as Paco leaned back. "Oh my God—that was so rude," Zach started apologizing.

Paco snarled and bit at Zach's hip—playfully. *For now.* I tensed. "No. It was delicious," he promised, and stood up.

Paco's jeans—Jack's jeans—were still on. And the way the overhead light was placed, I could see his hard on in the shadow he cast across the dining room floor, into the carpeted living room. I was sure from the front it was even more impressive.

Paco leaned forward, as if to whisper a secret to Zach, and I leaned forward too. Ears were close to necks, which were close to blood. "I want to fuck you," I heard him whisper, and then almost felt him kiss Zach's ear as if it were my own.

Zach shivered, then started kissing him back, fervently, as he divested himself of all his remaining clothes. Then he reached for Paco's belt and undid it, bowing before Paco as he helped him peel Jack's tight jeans off. Once Paco's cock was exposed, Zach paused.

"Condoms? Lube?" I asked, ever the good bloodslave.

"Bedside table on the left," Zach said, without even looking back.

I scampered off to get them and returned to find a fully naked Zach sucking on Paco's cock with all his might—and Paco looking dark and unholy, the storm again, personified. I ran up with a condom in hand and offered it out to Paco, glad when he took it because it meant that he was still *there*, his hunger wasn't in control of him yet. He wound his hand into Zach's hair and pushed the blond back, Zach's pursed lips still pulling as he was forced off, so Paco could lower the condom down between them. Zach, kneeling, helped him put it on, and then stared up with wide eyes, panting, knowing what Paco intended on doing with it.

"On your knees," Paco said with the tinge of command—I could feel it pull at me as well. Zach moved out to the carpet of his living room and sat just as I had, on so many nights, waiting to be taken.

Paco lowered himself behind him and started kissing Zach's back. Zach shivered each time Paco's lips touched him, and I wondered what it felt like for him—if some part of him knew the presence of greatness he was being kissed by. For my part, I tossed the bottle of lube over, and Paco caught it readily, without even looking up. I crawled over to one side waiting to see if I was needed —wanting to go along on the ride this time.

Paco rose up at long last, slicked his condomed cock with the lube before tossing it aside, and then tilted himself down with one hand, steadying himself on Zach's waist before beginning to push himself inside. Zach groaned as Paco moaned, whispering, "Fuck," to himself.

What was it like, as a vampire, to finally come into your own?

After surviving this night—would I finally get to know?

Paco started stroking softly, rubbing just his head in and out of Zach's ass, and Zach's groans kept time. My fingers darted between my legs—I was wet already, watching the two of them there was no way not to be, and I took some of that lubrication and swept it up to circle around my clit.

Paco pushed deeper, and deeper, I could see it from my vantage point, and hear it in Zach's voice, the pleasured sounds he was making as Paco's hard cock pushed faster, further, inside.

"Oh—there—there—fuck me there," Zach pleaded—and Paco did. He let his head roll back, his hips swinging metronomically, pounding himself into Zach, hard, as Zach brought a hand beneath him to stroke his own cock. My fingers rubbed harder, imagining getting fucked myself like that, sending racing bolts of fire through my hips and my nipples as I pulled at them. "You're gonna make me come again," Zach promised, his body arched, his face fierce with tension.

Paco growled, his jaw dropped, and fangs emerged.

Only I could see them. I didn't even know if Paco knew he had them—but Zach was going to feel them in a second. I rolled to a stand and ran over to them both, and swung my leg over Zach without thinking, so that I was standing facing Paco, blocking him from Zach. Paco snarled.

"Don't you dare stop," I told both of them. Paco's pace slowed and he looked at me with tragic eyes—the human part of him horrified at what he'd so easily become. "It's going to be okay, okay?" I told him, taking his head between my hands. "I won't let you hurt anyone," I mouthed to him, and then brought his mouth to my breast.

In retrospect, it was the stupidest thing I'd ever done. I didn't make a practice of martyring myself in general, so I don't know why I did it. I had killed people before, at Rosalie's command, and Zach meant nothing to me personally.

But some part of me knew that if I did this and lived, then Jack would truly owe me, in a way that he could never take back.

And another part of me was used to knowing I was going to die soon anyway, and not giving a singular solitary fuck.

Paco's fangs sank into my breast and I had to fight not to scream. It hurt—*it always hurt*—but while thrashing ahead of time and afterwards was fun, thrashing during was not really recommended. My blood poured into Paco's mouth as he silently stared up at me with dark eyes.

"Shh, shh," I counseled us both, trying to get a grip on my rising terror. Paco's hips had slowed, so Zach had taken things into his own hands, and was now thudding back onto Paco's cock, sending shockwaves up through him, into me. Paco's tongue worked against me roughly, turning me on as it coaxed more blood out and—

Usually with Rosalie I counted seconds. I'd had giving her blood down to an art. But with him—I blinked, feeling woozy. I'd lost track of time, and his mouth was bigger, he was sucking harder, and he wanted more, he was starving—I grabbed hold of the sides of his head, trying to pull him back. He snarled again.

"Paco," I whispered in warning, yanking on his hair and ears. "Stop it. You're hurting me," I said, so quiet only he could hear.

But whatever was human inside Paco was lost to me now.

"Paco," I said, in time with Zach's thuds and grunts below. "Paco!" I shouted—and then boxed his ears. He startled—first angry —but then his humanity returned to him, his fangs receded, and he looked at me, stunned, taking me in, the blood dripping from where he'd bitten me, realizing what he'd done.

"Oh God," he said.

"I know," Zach panted, still fucking Paco between my legs, beneath me. "Blow your load in me—please. I need it. I have to make you come."

Paco faced me, panting, eyes wide with horror, the taste of my blood in his mouth.

"Do it. You need it. Do it," I urged him. I caught the rest of my blood in a smear and pushed my fingers into his mouth. His lips sealed around them as he started thrusting again—and this time he and Zach were out of sync, which was all the better, as Zach threw himself back to be pinned onto Paco's hard cock, and the vampire that'd bitten me moaned low.

"Fuck him like you mean it," I said, pulling my fingers safely out. Paco reached around me to grab Zach and pulled himself deep.

"*Come.*" It was the first time he'd used his *voice* since being reborn earlier this evening. "*Come, come, come,*" he commanded, louder, feeling his power—and Zach and I did, helplessly.

Zach shouted below us, I could feel him writhing, knew that he was jetting his cum into his hand, whereas I collapsed against Paco, throwing my arms around his neck, shouting and trembling on my toes, as the orgasm I'd been denied earlier flew through my body and into his, waves of it, just like he commanded, again and again.

"Yes—*God*—yes," Paco growled, feeling our power leave us and fill him. His face was pressed against my breasts. His tongue savagely licked the smear of blood he'd left behind, and then he took me physically with him when he came into Zach, his hips thrusting hard as his body arced down, all of him spasming as he shot out his load, just like Zach had asked him.

For a second, we were all sweaty and tangled, like we'd played the world's best game of Twister—and then Zach collapsed forward, and I would've fallen if Paco hadn't caught me. He held me where I stood, panting as his tongue and lips licked blood from me, unthinking. I played a hand through his hair, wondering if and when it would be safe to move.

"Oh my God," Zach whispered from below. His frank humanity startled both of us and made everything easier. I pulled back—thanks to Paco's tongue I could hide the wound with a hand—and stepped over him, to go throw myself back into his dining room chair. Zach looked back at Paco over his shoulder like he was a dark god. "That was amazing," he said, pushing hair out of his face.

"Yeah—it was," Paco agreed, catching his breath, pulling himself out of Zach's ass and slipping the condom free. I could almost see him thinking how much more life he could wring from Zach—and wondering if it would be enough. I stood to stop him before he could go for round three. There was a point at which there were diminishing returns, and if Jack was back and had a better plan—but when I moved too quickly, it made the floor swim.

"Zach—thank you so much," I told him, trying to keep calm.

Zach rolled his hands down his chest to grab his cock and cup his own balls, as if in disbelief over what they'd done. "I can't claim to understand any of this. But goddamn if it doesn't feel good."

Paco chuckled and I could see him considering falling forward and pinning the younger man there again. Paco knew how vampires worked from being with Jack—if he wanted to he could be hard again and again and again. Zach grinned up, so damn wholesome it hurt, and reached up for him. God, if they started fucking again there was no way I'd be able to drag Paco free—but somehow Paco realized that, and rocked back to standing. Somehow I managed to sweep up Jack's jeans without falling and shake them at him. "Let's get going."

"Oh, come on," Zach said, rolling over, tucking his hand underneath his head to hold himself up. "Jack's never come up here. You haven't even seen my bed."

Paco walked into the kitchen and tossed his full condom in the trash—and took the jeans from my hands. "Sorry, kid. Another time."

"Kid?" Zach protested, gathering himself up. "I'm not some kid—I'm not someone you can just leave behind."

"Wipe him," I told Paco. Things were blurry. I had to concentrate. Just how much blood had I lost? *Shit, shit, shit.* I pulled on my shirt, and yanked up my skirt again. "Do it."

"How?" Paco asked, over Zach's further protests.

"Tell him he won't remember you—or me. Say it like you mean it." Paco looked at me and frowned. "Look, everything else was consensual, okay? We're dealing with some extenuating circumstances, you and I."

Zach was standing now. "What the fuck are you talking about?"

Paco turned. He inhaled, and then hesitated, clearly feeling torn.

"Goddammit, you are just like him!" I complained and looked to Zach myself. "Don't say anything about this, okay? We were never here." My voice didn't have any magic weight behind it to keep him silent, but by the time Zach was done sputtering about our dismissal, Paco had collected all his clothes.

"I'm not a kid!" he protested again.

"No, you're not, but you're also lucky to be alive," I snarled, herding Paco into the hall, where he finished pulling on his jeans.

He watched me with dark eyes as he tugged his shirt on. "How many times could Jack have wiped me?" he asked.

"You can ask him when we see him," I said, and started walking back downstairs.

CHAPTER TWENTY-ONE
JACK

Maya's attendants brought the Sangre Rojo emissaries back as the lights dimmed. Maya had taken a place upon the dias and was lounging on a ridiculously gilded chair—but there was a spotlight on her, which made her red hair shimmer and the jewels on all her fingers glint. Her gold beaded dress cast out blinding sparks of light beneath the fur coat she also wore.

She looked positively regal which I supposed was good, and in front of her Zevvi, her bloodslave, was apparently willingly chained.

There were ten Rojo in all, each one of them better dressed than the last, wearing suits with pinstripes, flat hats, and pocket squares, five and five on each side of some sort of structure covered by black velvet, I could tell by the way the light rippled on it. When they were done presenting themselves, the tallest one moved forward.

"The loyal Rojo present themselves at the Red Dancer's behest," he said, bowing to Maya with a flourish. "I am Arnulfo."

"I am Maya, and this is Jack. Welcome to our home. You may come in," Maya said, standing to gesture them forward.

"We are grateful for the hospitality," he said. Maya stepped down the dais to stand beside Zevvi, as the Rojo wheeled their structure nearer. "We were saddened to learn of the loss of your matriarch—but not entirely surprised."

Maya shrugged one shoulder. "Just because one can live forever doesn't guarantee it."

A smile flickered across Arnulfo's lips. "Indeed. Do you have what we desire?"

Maya tilted her head, sending a cascade of red across her fur. "I have what every man desires."

He laughed. "In that case then, do you have the deed?"

"I do." Maya pouted, and reached into her fur. I watched all the Rojo tense, prepared for subterfuge. They were used to fighting—and had brought a small army. I glanced around the room to Maya's people and saw them thinking the same thing—if this went bad, they'd all surely die.

How many people was Sam bringing? And what the hell time was it?

Maya brought out a sheaf of paper and the Rojo relaxed. "Your money reached my accounts yesterday. And so this is now yours." She rolled the papers into a wand, handing them over like a baton.

The lead Rojo took them, unfurled them, and grunted while reading. "Excellent. We appreciate doing business with you. Your matriarch was," he began, and Maya held up her hand.

"Let us not speak ill of the dead, when we could be drinking from the living."

He nodded and snapped his fingers. "Of course."

One of the Rojo behind him pulled down the black velvet curtain, revealing an absolutely beautiful woman completely naked and elaborately chained upright, as though she were trapped on a silver spider's web—and I recognized her.

Camila. The woman I'd fucked earlier on in the night.

She saw me spot her— and winked.

I was so stunned by that, I almost didn't see the way Maya's head turned for a moment, as though she were listening to someone else speak.

"I have heard many stories of the dark delights within these walls," Arnulfo said, walking slowly forward to where Zevvi waited. She'd stripped herself before locking in, and the spot-light Maya had left behind was half on her, looking like the light itself was taking a bite of her naked flesh.

"As I have heard many stories of the Rojo's delicious women," Maya agreed, returning her full attention to the current situation and walking to Camila's side. "As I take blood from you and yours," Maya began.

"It is as if you drink my blood from me," Arnulfo finished for her. As one they both bent down to proffered humans and I saw Camila wince as Zevvi made a helpless sound.

Everything else in the room was completely still while Maya and Arnulfo drank.

When you drank—you were vulnerable. Just like a shark. There was no way for you to react in time to danger—no way to clearly see. Even the one you were drinking from could attack you. It was why so many incompetent vampires killed their prey, just for safety.

But Arnulfo had his squad of Rojo looking on and Maya had me. They watched me with singular intent and glittering eyes, and I did my best to simultaneously watch all of them. Zevvi squirmed and I didn't know if it was meaningful or not, if he was drinking too hard and hurting her, or if it was one of the many lures surely Rosalie's bloodslaves had learned to please their Mistress.

Whichever it was—Arnulfo raised his head with a wide and bloody grin. "Your blood is charming," he told Maya.

For her part, Maya had carefully bitten into the meat of Camila's exposed breast, and had expertly stroked the woman's breast as she sucked for greater blood flow. Camila had writhed in the chains in response, and the scent of her sex was in the air, familiar to me from earlier in the night.

"As is yours," Maya said, rising up, daintily dabbing at the corners of her mouth.

Arnulfo turned toward Maya. "I would take her with me." Behind him Zevvi twisted her head to look to beg Maya for protection with fearful eyes.

"I apologize, but she is a personal favorite. My offering her was an honor. "

"Nonsense," Arnulfo said, looking back down. "No one's blood is more important than business." He brushed a lock of Zevvi's hair from her face, clearly enjoying her panic. "Your matriarch taught me that. I am surprised she did not manage to teach you."

Maya stiffened.

"If you have things you want to keep," he went on, "then you do not bring them out and show them. Or you bring an army, if you do," he said, gesturing at Camila and his men. "So. Lesson learned. Give me the girl, and we will leave you, business finished."

He'd put Maya in an impossible situation. If she angered the Rojo, we were clearly outnumbered—*so far*—and we might all die. If she let him take Zevvi, she would lose face in front of all of her slaves —and what was to stop each of his men from claiming their own girl after that? Concession was a slippery slope.

Maya shifted, staring at the ground a moment as if contrite. "Haven't we done enough business already?" she asked, her voice the soul of innocence. She let the fur fall from her shoulders, revealing the dress she wore beneath—embroidered with gold beads in a snake scale pattern, it was the same color as the setting sun, and it rode her curves from her shoulders to ankles like a second skin. She took a step toward Arnulfo. "Why take her—when you could take me?"

His eyes narrowed. "We are Rojo. We take what we desire."

Maya's lips pulled into a mysterious smile. "What if I desire you? What do I get to take?" Arnulfo had clearly not been expecting this turn of events—and neither had I. I had no idea what game Maya was playing at, and wondered if this was her way of killing time.

Maya's fingers reached for the beads riding just above her stomach, and pulled the dress off of her skin before tearing it. Every single eye in the room was on her as beads began spilling quietly to the floor.

"I've never been with another vampire before," she said. "Rosalie wouldn't let me."

And that was a lie. Rosalie had thrown Maya in with me just after I'd been turned. I knew Maya was playing now—I looked around with just my eyes, because moving might break the spell she was creating—and saw the cameras Rosalie had kept an eye on her club with disappear into their corners, and watched gun barrels emerge instead.

How many bloodslaves did Rosalie and Maya have combined? I didn't know—but I strongly suspected not all of them were down here.

"All my life—my unlife, really—Rosalie kept me caged," Maya went on, continuing to tear her exquisite dress until the opening reached the ground, beads raining down like hourglass sand. "But now I'm free. At long last. And I want to soar." She kicked off both of her shoes to be shorter and less threatening and took another step near him, the slit she'd created in her dress showing everything she had to offer. No underwear—and nothing was hidden, beneath a trimmed patch of red curls. "I want to finally know what it would be like to be with a man who could handle me."

Arnulfo looked disparaging. "Here?"

Maya puckered her lips into an impish grin. "No one from the Red Dancer's nest is ever shy." She canted her hips so that one leg struck out through the impossibly high tear, and glanced past him at the wall of Rojo beyond. "I think I could take two or three of you, honestly. And then some of my girls could service the rest—and we would all be so...well...fed." She punctuated herself by tapping down his chest, and then turning her hand to push it down over his cock, rubbing him through his suit.

"You're trying to use me," he said.

"Only to get off," she agreed and gave him a *look*. "But why ever would you mind?"

He caught her wrist. She looked pained and the entire room tensed as he yanked her arm high, and then spun her so that her arm was hitched up high behind her back. "Did you expect me to take you seriously?" he whispered as she kicked. "No woman is ever the equal of us." He grabbed hold of a fistful of hair and pulled her neck back. "I will fuck you over that ridiculous chair and bleed you," he said. I could see the black shine of an earpiece in her ear now with her hair out of the way, and as he hauled her past me I could see her mouthing the word NOW.

Maya didn't have to tell me twice. I leaned down, pulled out my silver boot knife, and threw it at him, hard enough to make sure it cut his spine.

He tensed for a moment, as if he couldn't believe this was happening to him, and then started to dissipate. After that, the remaining Rojo crew shouted, guns started shooting, and chaos reigned.

CHAPTER TWENTY-TWO
LUNA

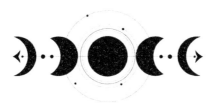

It was twelve. Jack was not back yet and Paco was stalking around his small apartment like a caged animal.

"Are you okay?" I asked him, edging toward the door.

"No. You?" Paco asked.

I'd raided Jack's extremely limited pantry and was drinking coffee so black it was almost sludge, hoping the sheer quantity of caffeine would constrict my veins. "Honestly—no."

"I didn't mean to," Paco started. I held up my hand.

"You didn't know any better."

"Where is he? Why isn't he back yet?"

"He didn't think you'd be up till three." I swallowed. "If he really does take that long, do you think you can make it?"

He didn't answer me. Which was, in and of itself, an answer.

"That's what I thought." I didn't think I could make it to three, either. *Come on, bone marrow. Churn out some blood cells. Get pumping.* "All right. New plan. I know where he is. We'll go to meet him."

"Good," Paco said.

"Hope you don't mind driving," I said, grabbing my bag and tossing him my keys.

PACO LOOKED ridiculous behind the wheel of my Fiat. I'd brought my car with me the first night of course, and parked it far away so Jack wouldn't think I had one. All the better to guilt him into giving me rides—but neither Paco nor I could risk using an Uber tonight. Besides, it wasn't like I could get into more trouble than I was currently in, constantly on the verge of fainting around a starving vampire.

"Where are we going?" Paco asked, putting the car in drive.

"Vermillion. Have you been there before?"

"Reluctantly," he said, and we took off.

I WAS FADING against the window when Paco asked, "What's Jack gotten himself into now?"

I pushed myself upright and took several deep breaths. "I'm not entirely sure. He's helping Maya, another vampire."

He looked over. "The one that beat me?"

"Oh no. No, no, no. Maya helped Jack kill Rosalie. *She* was the one that tried to kill you for revenge." At this, Paco grunted. "He wouldn't be helping Maya unless it was important," I went on. If I kept talking, I'd stay awake.

"It had better be," Paco said, his voice dark.

"He didn't just forget about you, you know. He died beside you every morning."

Paco didn't say anything, but his hands wrung the steering wheel a bit tighter.

AS WE TURNED onto the road that led to Vermillion, I could see its familiar cursive sign—and watch the way the 'V' was blinking in imperfect semaphore.

"Oh shit," I muttered.

"What?" Paco looked over.

"They're in trouble. The light, it means all hands on deck."

"You're sure he didn't say anything?"

"He wouldn't tell me." Except he sort of had with his question about the Rojo. Why else would Jack have asked it? *Oh God.* "Wait. I think they're meeting with another vampire nest tonight—doing business."

"I take it vampires don't play nice with one another?"

"Not usually." As we neared, I saw Vermillion's parking lot was full of pristine vintage cars—and nearby parked unmarked white vans. "Don't pull in—get down," I said, shrinking myself lower. "We'll park up the street."

Paco did as he was told, and we both slunk out, closing our doors quietly. "Those aren't party vans," I said, once we were outside.

"Good eye."

"Give me my keys again—there's a way in the back." I held my hand out. It wobbled unsteadily.

"I think you should wait here."

I stared him down—all three of him. "Fuck that. I know the layout inside. Plus I know the rules. You don't know shit, except you almost accidentally killed me, so give me the goddamned keys."

His jaw clenched, but he handed the keyring over.

"Okay. It's this one," I said, without showing him. "Just—carry me over. Quietly. To the back."

Without preamble, he scooped me up, and started jogging near the fenceline.

THERE WERE three doors at the back of Vermillion—the delivery door, the girls' exit/entrance, and the third door, which only Rosalie's favorites knew, which looked like an electrician's service panel and led to the secret tunnel where my Master had taken me for the first time. Only I and my predecessor with Rosalie had had the key. Paco set me down, I popped the lock—and then I heard: *"Hold,"* inside my head.

I turned, lunging for my bag, and found Paco already with his hands up. We were surrounded by a squad of people—Faithful—dressed in white, and holding an assortment of weapons, from daggers to machine guns. Sam was at the head of them.

"What're you doing here?" I held my bag between me and her, prepared to swing it, hoping the nightblade's repellent action worked through canvas.

"Tonight we are on the same side," she whispered.

"Like hell we are." Jack would never put in with the Faithful—would he? Maya knew better, at least.

"Your man requested our protection," Sam said, with her light accent.

"Jack?" Paco asked, voice full of concern—and I knew I was sunk.

"The same," Sam said, her eyes flicking over him, judging him.

"He is *my* man," Paco said, correcting her. "And I didn't sign on for this to lose him."

Sam turned to look back at her crew. None of them fought her. "Okay," she said. "But we do things on my count."

"Too bad I'm the only one with—" I began.

"Give me the key," Paco commanded me—remembering that he could at last.

"Goddammit!" I protested, as my body obeyed and handed it over.

THE FAITHFUL AVOIDED me in the tunnels which was fine, and Paco ran ahead with Sam. There was a lock on the far door, but I had a feeling they would just burst through, a feeling which was confirmed when I got there and found the door hanging—able to hear fighting in the rooms beyond.

I wanted to go in and help but I was becoming all too aware of my current mortality. I sat down against a crate of barware, cold and shivering, feeling increasingly unwell. Would my current Master save me? Would anyone notice me before I died?

To do all this for nothing. To come this far and still be denied.

To be in this goddamned same tunnel and have my dreams die again, only this time in a far more permanent fashion....

I fished inside my bag and brought out the nightblade, dipping in and out of consciousness, hovering in the present, falling into my past—remembering the first time Rosalie saw me. How I'd felt when she pulled me out of a crowd of dancers to tell me that I danced beautifully. Of course I did—I'd spent my entire childhood studying ballet. She dared me to spin for her, and I did—I spun so hard I spun into her bed—

The door at the end opened up, casting everything in bright white light and a shadow ran at me.

"Rosalie?" I whispered.

The shadow paused, apparently surprised. A face peered down. I didn't recognize her—and she wasn't wearing white.

"No witnesses," she muttered and lifted a heavy glass with intent —so without thinking I slashed at her with the nightblade.

The jagged edge caught her across her chest and she cried out in pain as I felt the spatter of warm blood. The blade didn't hurt her like it had Sam—whoever she was, she wasn't 'good'—but I could feel its pleasure radiating up my hand nonetheless, like it'd been thirsty and it wanted more.

Meanwhile what little blood I had left in me was surging, focused on keeping this sad and perpetually disappointing meat-body alive. I pulled myself to a crouch as she looked from her gouged chest to me, her face curdling in anger. "Stay back," I growled, shaking the nightblade at her, feeling like a caveman.

"Fuck you!" she shouted, and ran for me.

CHAPTER TWENTY-THREE
JACK

The sound of the guns was deafening and the Rojo were fucking pissed.

My silver knife was lost in Arnulfo's back, and three of the Rojo were coming for me. The first one I dodged, the second one I gut-punched, and the third—I just went for his balls, using them to pick him up in the air and chucked him across the room, hopefully through a bullet's path. Two Rojo got picked off by a mounted gun while running for the exits—confirming that Maya was rocking silver ammo—but those gun's range were limited by the slots they were forced to shoot through—so all they could really control was the main door. The mounted guns kept up steady bursts, and I wondered how many Rojo were outside, trying to get in.

A Rojo came up on me with a knife. I sidestepped him, grabbed his wrist, bowled him over, and found Maya, half-naked, fighting just as hard as I was beside me.

"Where's your fucking help?" she shouted at me, wading through the Rojo, trying to save her people.

"Don't know!" I shouted back, wondering if the Faithful had left us here to die.

Her bloodslaves were performing admirably under the certain death circumstances, but I'd heard more than one scream end poorly, and could scent the fresh blood in the room. They'd boosted the seat cushions inside the alcoves and pulled out weaponry—but Maya was too smart to give a nearby human a silver-loaded gun, so they were reduced to shooting at creatures like myself who were nigh unstoppable, filling them full of lead.

Maya pounced on a Rojo whose back was turned, twisting his head clean off, but there were still five of them left—five and a half, if you counted the one sucking all the blood out of a corpse, trying to heal himself from a gaping chest wound. Another spotted Zevvi, still trapped, and started lurching for her on half a leg.

"Oh no, you don't." I leaned over and caught the back of his suit, throwing him down and stomping on his neck until I'd severed his head from his body. Then I ran to her and hoisted the nearest table up, flipping it carefully over her, hopefully giving her slightly more cover.

As I turned I saw the few Rojo who'd been missing in action—guarding Camila I'd assumed—finish whatever it was they were doing. She dropped free, still draped in metal—while they hauled up the board she'd been strapped and ran over to use it as a bullet-block to help the Rojo waiting outside get in the door. Maya saw what I was seeing and shouted, "Fuck!" at the top of her lungs—just as Faithful started pouring in from somewhere behind me, Sam at their head.

"Jack," said a familiar voice.

I turned and Paco was there. My Paco. The man who'd saved me, once upon a time—the man I loved. I stepped over a dusted Rojo's corpse and kissed him, hard, pressing all of my body against his, needing to feel him, smell him, taste him, right now.

And then I heard a gunshot and felt a stabbing pain flow through my body and into Paco's. I whirled and saw Maya with a gun. She'd fucking shot me on purpose—and through me, Paco—comingling our blood. "Jesus-Christ-now-is-not-the-time, Jack!" she shouted.

Paco touched where the bullet had hit him, where he was bleeding, and looked at the blood, then at me. "Do you need some help with all this?"

"The fuckers in the suits need to die, but try not to kill any humans."

Paco rose up on his toes. He'd been a martial arts expert and bodyguard in his former life—he knew ways to kill people I hadn't even dreamed of. "Copy that," he said and ran into the fray.

"If you fucking shoot him I will make you watch me eat you!" I threatened whomever was running the overhead guns, then ran in after him.

I HOPED—ASSUMED—THAT the Faithful were stemming the flow of Rojo back into the outside world, because all of a sudden their numbers became finite, and then started to dwindle, as Paco tore ruthlessly through enemies. I paused in my own fighting to watch him; it was like watching a dancer dance, the way he flowed back and forth, precisely striking before regathering himself to strike again. I knew he'd been good at his job before, but my gift of vampirism had made him glorious.

I surveyed the room. The staccato of the overhead guns had stopped—this room was ours—and it sounded like the next was becoming so, too.

"Jack?" I heard a nervous voice call my name, and crouched to find its owner. Camila, my lay from earlier in the evening, crouched naked, eyes wide.

"For the record, I always knew you were a professional," I said. I reached a hand out to her, and she timidly took it, letting me help her stand. The chains they'd left around her complimented her figure, hitting at her neck, waist, and ankle.

Then, from the next room, the sound of Sam's voice was a

demanding shout. "Jack!" I tensed, and grabbed Camila, putting her over my shoulder for safekeeping.

I ran into the next room with the main stage and found the Faithful were arranged around the stage like so many patrons, all staring intently up at where Paco had gotten the best of one of them. One of the Faithful was glowing, another held bolts of fire, a third was breathing mist, and several chairs were hovering nearby Sam.

Paco had a very young man, all dressed in white, pressed against him, both of them facing forward, both of them breathing hard. I could see Paco fighting to stay in control—and how the delicious fear of the Faithful boy was making that hard for him.

"It's his first night!" I shouted as an explanation and dropped Camila to the ground, hearing her squeal as she landed.

My first night had involved a lot of fighting—but I'd been able to eat everyone I'd fought. Even then there'd been a period of time I'd blacked out for, when my hunger had ruled me without conscious thought. Poor Paco'd spent the last fifteen minutes killing Rojos who turned to dust—it was amazing that he'd bested his hunger this long. I leapt up on the stage, bodily blocking him from their weapons, and Paco snarled at me as I landed, like a dog growling over a bone, unable to speak with his fangs.

"I know you're hungry," I said, "but there's plenty of food here, Paco. Set the boy down."

Paco pulled the boy away from me and growled again. I could feel the tension ratchet in the room, as all the watching Faithful leaned in.

"I know. I know. You're hungry. I get it." I still remembered what it felt like, how I'd found myself suddenly starving. I wished there was a way I could make it easier for Paco, and honestly promise him that it would end. "But we're surrounded by those who would give blood and more, willingly. There's no need to taste him. He's not one of ours."

Paco held the boy tighter. No one had ever tried to reason with me when I'd been slaughtering—I didn't know what it was like. But I did know Paco. He was a reasonable man. Despite his capacity for violence, he didn't believe in it for its own sake.

I looked out to the people on the ground, past the Faithful. Trust Luna to not be here the only time I'd ever wanted her—and I didn't see Camila anymore, goddammit—but the girl I'd saved, Zevvi, was watching from the doorway. I reached out a hand for her, and she leaned back into the other room for a moment before responding. Then she threaded through the Faithful, followed by the five other bloodslaves she'd convinced. One by one they mounted the stage, and I could hear the mutters of the Faithful as we became a wall of bodies, blocking Paco from their possible revenge.

Zevvi looked at me. She was already pale from earlier in the night. "Stay close?" she asked quietly.

"Of course," I said, and took the wrist of the man next to me, offering him to Paco instead.

I could see Paco sway with the effort of becoming himself again —a creature intelligent enough to know a better choice—and there was a glimmer of his old self in his eyes. I stepped forward and put my hands on the boy, while the bloodslave next to me bravely kept his wrist out, even though it was trembling.

"Please, Paco. We've got this. Let us help you."

I gently pried the Faithful boy free—and felt Paco's urges move on to the man next to me instead, one of Maya's. He grabbed the wrist and pulled the man in, his back to Paco's chest, as if they were about to dance. Paco's eyes were closed and I knew he was fighting an internal battle.

"What's your name?" I asked the bloodslave.

"Kel," he responded.

"Kel—Paco. Paco—Kel. We don't eat people whose names we know, all right?"

Kel flashed me a brave smile, then reached up, running his fingers through Paco's hair to bring Paco's mouth down on his neck.

Paco's teeth sank inside as Kel panted, and I would've sworn I heard my lover purr.

At that, the spell was broken—the bloodslaves knew what they were doing more than I did—one of them unbuckled Kel's pants and took his cock into their mouth, whereas one of the women started grinding up on Zevvi. I realized those who weren't feeding him blood would be feeding him life in other ways shortly. I wouldn't leave his side, I'd promised them, but I did turn around, to find several of the Faithful watching, rapt, while others averted their eyes.

Just how pure did pure have to be?

Sam stood in front of the boy Paco had captured earlier. It was telling that he'd ran to her for protection.

"Sorry about that. He's new, as of today."

"We'll start his file then." Her voice was dry and clinical. I couldn't help but look around and realize the distinct imbalance of power in the room. We'd killed all the Rojo together, but what bound us now? Did Faithful really believe in honor amongst thieves? "His name is Paco, you said?"

"It is."

"Are you planning on making more vampires?"

My answer was interrupted by Maya's return. She had Camila over her shoulder, same as I had earlier, and dropped the girl to the floor—only this time, she had a jagged cut across her chest and a black eye.

The sounds of someone orgasming behind me, and Paco's subsequent satisfied groan, made me feel a little more safe for the bloodslaves' lives—that, and they'd switched Paco's donor out. I dared to hop off the edge of the stage, while always keeping an eye on it, and walked over to Maya.

She was covered in streaks of torn satin, dust, blood, and the raiment of her hair, and I could tell she took pleasure from the horrified way many of the Faithful were now watching her blunt nudity. She dusted a sheaf of papers off on her thigh, before offering it to Sam.

"I believe these are yours now," Maya said. "Needless to say, you and I will ever meet again."

Samantha walked forward, but paused as though she were listening inside, which was strange until I remembered she was telepathic. She took the papers from Maya, but then looked at the girl.

"What are you going to do with her?"

"Please, rescue me, take me with you," Camila began, weeping openly.

"I can tell you what I'd like to do with her," Maya said. "She's Rojo. I caught her almost beating your bloodslave to death."

My bloodslave? Oh God—how had Paco gotten here? Only Luna could've told him where I was, and I hadn't seen her yet tonight.

"The Rojo," Camila said, touching her ragged chest to show her blood to Sam. "They will not take me back. I will be scarred—I am cursed!"

Maya squatted beside her. "Don't worry, girl. I can think of many uses for you," she purred. Camila's eyes widened—as did Sam's. I reached down and caught Camila's hair, yanking her up to face me, remembering fucking her earlier in the night. They'd clearly sent her into the club at the Fleur de Lis, to offer a tempting distraction to me.

"Go back to your clan and tell them that the Faithful came with an army and interrupted the bargain. There were heavy casualties on both sides. You only barely made it out alive. Throw yourself on their mercy, should they have any," I said, and pushed her toward Vermillion's door. She turned back, gawking and confused, but then ran for it.

"Jack," Maya complained, frowning after the departing girl without following. There was another satisfied gasp from the stage, and I could feel the dregs of a distant orgasm flitter through me, like the smallest sip of fine wine.

"She'll go back to them and tell them what happened here. The Faithful don't kill innocent humans, right? So she'll say they set her free. And when she gets there, she'll be a warning. We have to have someone on the inside tell our side of the story."

CHAPTER TWENTY-THREE

"But the Rojo will abandon her," Sam said, her jaw clenched.

Camila was telling the truth? "Will they kill her?"

"I don't know."

Another imposing Faithful came up, a man, short and wide—the one I'd seen holding flames earlier. He nodded to Sam before speaking out loud for our sake. "It is not like she could've become one of us and it's not like we could've left her here."

Maya sniffed. "Here is a perfectly fine place to be." I glanced back at the stage. Paco was caught in a tangle of limbs now, and the scent of sex was thick in the air. Soon I would get to take my turn and we need never be separated again.

"I'm partial to it myself," I said, tearing my eyes away slowly. "That land is yours now, to do with as you see fit. Are we done here tonight?"

Sam twisted back and took a moment to check in with each of her followers mentally.

"We are," Sam agreed.

"Until next time then," Maya said, ready to whammy them all out the door. Sam's lips lifted into a hint of a smile and then turned away, leading the rest of the Faithful out in a single file line. Maya watched them go, then whirled on me. "I cannot believe that worked."

"Neither can I."

"You missed a promising career as a gambler, Jack," she said, setting a fallen chair upright then falling into it.

I rose up on my toes, listening to the sounds of the orgy still occurring on the stage. Now that the Faithful were gone, even more bloodslaves were joining in. "Is Luna okay?"

"Yes, no thanks to you."

I hesitated, pulled between what I likely ought to do—check on Luna, who I owed—and what I wanted to do. Maya watched my indecision with a smug pout. "She's asleep anyhow," Maya said, absolving me.

"Thank you," I told her, then turned for the stage.

ALMOST ALL THEIR clothing was cast aside and it felt like it would be rude if I didn't ditch mine also, when I joined them. So I took my time, undressing myself, as though I were at the edge of a hidden pool, full of bodies instead of water.

Once I was naked, with all of my many tattoos showing, I dove in.

Women and men groped me without thinking and I welcomed their attention. A hand reached for my thigh, while I cupped someone's breast—a mouth met my mouth and kissed me like we were drowning. Skin touched skin touched skin. There was no shame, not in taking what you wanted, nor in offering it to be taken. I crawled through the throng, kissing, caressing, feeling a hot hand reach out for my hanging cock, stroking it as I pulled away.

And in the center of it all was Paco. He was halfway naked now, on his back, a man clasped to his chest, his cock in their ass, fucking him as I used to fuck him, with his mouth on the man's neck—while someone else leaned in to stroke the bloodslave's cock. I gently took their place, replacing their hand with my own, feeling the bloodslave writhe in pleasure as Paco pinned him. I leaned over to kiss the man, startling him, before I made him groan with my hand, and pulled my head back.

Paco pulled back as well, his mouth rimed with blood, and his fangs receded—for now. He stared at me with heavy lidded eyes. "Is this always what it's like?"

"Not always. But sometimes," I whispered, leaning in to kiss him.

I could taste the bloodslave's blood as Paco kissed me passionately and felt as he started to fuck the bloodslave harder. I stroked the bloodslave's cock in time, watching his face wind up, as other orgasms exploded all around us, like we were in the middle of an unrelenting firework show. The bloodslave started crying out as I made him spurt warm cum, and Paco stopped kissing me to shove the man down and filled his ass with a shout. Paco's head rolled back, his whole body shuddering, feeling the experience head to toe, his own orgasm atop the many happening all around him.

I leaned over to kiss his neck and ear. "My turn," I whispered, gently pushing the spent bloodslave aside, and Paco gasped, twisting his head to look at me.

"Yes," he agreed, he kissed me again, and I didn't know which way we would go next—but then he turned, presenting his back and ass. I wrapped my arms around him tightly. To think all those days I'd spent in the coffin with him like this, only to now have them repaid with this—I took my time kissing his neck and shoulders, my hard cock wedged between the cleft of his ass, just taking pleasure in the fact that Paco, *my Paco*, was alive.

But it had been too long—and this was Paco's night. Everyone here had a duty to feed him through it—even me. Paco moved a little, rubbing himself against me like a cat. I bit his shoulder to warn him, then reached between us, lining my cock up, stroking the tip of it against him. Even though he was a vampire now and as magnificent as I was, I still wanted him to beg.

"Jack," he complained, almost a laugh, his voice soft. I wrapped an arm around his chest from below, my other arm down across his hips from above and thrust.

His ass took me so smoothly. It was like I was meant to be there —because I was. No one's ass had ever brought me as much pleasure as Paco's had before—and now that he was with me—I would take him to such great heights.

"Oh God," Paco whispered, tensing around me.

"Do you remember our first time like this?" I asked in a whisper. He nodded.

"Then don't thank God—thank me," I said, and began to thrust.

I MADE PACO COME, and come, and come again, wrapping my body around his, making him take me, the head of my cock drumming his spot deep inside. He would tense, gasp, shout, pause, and then I would need him more. It was like each time he came he made me hungrier for him, until I was the one who was starving and needed it. The bodies swirled around us—humans were coming behind us, Maya was being eaten out as she sucked off another bloodslave a short distance away, and a girl I barely recognized offered Paco a dripping wrist which he drank from desperately in between bouts of ecstasy.

The sound, the smell, the feel of him around me—all of that was almost too much, and I was on the edge of coming myself, losing myself inside him again, all the way. And this time, knowing he was back in my arms, for always, that I would never have to set him free —I bit his shoulder, for real now, staking my claim. He was mine. I was his. I reached around and started stroking until he was hard again, as I fucked him harder and he sensed the change in me, crooning my name in long moans, opening his ass deeper, wider, so that there was no part of him I did not know—until I pulled him to me bodily and shouted his name, "Paco!" I came inside of him in a violent spasm, as he came too, curving forward, dragging me with him, feeling his cum spurt out against my hand.

I gasped behind him, catching my breath, kissing him, never wanting this to end, wanting the spend the rest of my life right here, just fucking him. But then I saw Maya was standing nearby, looking just as sex-drugged as I felt. Bloodslaves were now stumbling off the stage, going to wherever it was they slept off anemia and sex hang-overs.

"All right, boys. I've offered more than enough hospitality this evening."

She was right. I had to get me and mine home before dawn. I slid out of Paco with a sigh and heard him groan in agreement. But he was himself now—we'd abated the hunger, for tonight. He stood and it was hard not to think about mauling him again. How would I manage to keep my hands off of him all the way home? Would Luna be well enough to drive?

My eyes traveled up his body—and when my gaze reached his face I could see reality catching up with him. "Jack," he whispered, looking down at himself, realizing everything he'd done.

I sobered up instantly. "I know. It's a lot to take in."

"What happened to Kristopher? Does he know?" Paco's expression furrowed with concern. "What does he think happened to me? And—my business—what happened with that?"

Kristopher was Paco's long-term monogamish magician boyfriend. I was just supposed to be Paco's side-piece—like he was mine. When one of us had been a vampire and the other a human, it was the only way it could be.

"It's only been three days," I said, trying to downplay things.

"He must be worried," Paco said.

"He doesn't know what you are now, Paco. And honestly, I don't think you should tell him."

Paco swallowed. "I'm not going to *not* give the man closure. We lived together—I have to get my things—I owe him that."

Maya cleared her throat. "Excuse me, gentlemen, but it is almost dawn."

Paco moved to the side of the stage and started pulling on his clothing. I went after him. "You know I was just trying to help, Paco. Then—and now."

Paco looked at me, his eyes dark. "I know. But you're right—this is a lot."

I put myself in his path. "Which is why I don't want you to go through it alone."

He paused and kissed me, and for a blissful second I thought all was forgiven, until he pulled back. "I remember how you lived back then. I know how to do that."

"Paco," I protested.

"I'll be okay. I just need to figure out some things."

I leaned forward. I wanted to argue with him—and I had never been more tempted to whammy him in my life. I was his maker—his Master, technically—which meant even though we were both vampires, I could do that. I could make him do anything I wanted.

I just couldn't make him be mine.

"Okay," I said, nodding reluctantly. "You know where to find me."

"I do," he said, swallowing. He looked for a second more like he might kiss me—then jumped off the stage and walked for the door.

I TURNED, and found Maya watching. Her expression let me know what she thought of our exchange. "You are no Rosalie," she said.

"You say that like it's a bad thing," I quipped, sounding lighter than I felt. "Where's Luna?"

"In the back," she said. "I'll show you."

I followed Maya to a room full of bunk beds holding bloodslaves like they were at some vampire summer camp. "Really?" I asked her, but she didn't answer me. Only some of them turned to look at us, most of them were already snoring.

Maya led me through to the back, where there was a communal bathroom set with toilets and open shower stalls, and Luna, on the floor, with an almost empty IV bag of normal saline hanging off of a robe hook, with a long plastic line dangling down to her arm.

"What's this for?" I asked, but I already knew the answer. Luna was normally pale and goth—but now she looked almost translucent. Blood loss, likely due to Paco—and what little blood she did have was creating lovely bruises on her head and around her neck.

"I found that Rojo bloodslave strangling her with a chain. Luna was trying to stop her. With this," Maya said, holding out the strange bone weapon Luna'd used against Sam. "You ever see this before?"

"No," I lied. "You?"

"Nope."

"Maybe Rosalie gave it to her?" At least that's what Luna had implied the other night.

Maya gave me a bemused look. "Our Rosalie?" she said, and laughed. She was still laughing as she disconnected Luna from the IV line, easily picking her up to hand her over. "If she's going to die, she can die at your place today." I took her, and Maya tossed the piece of bone onto Luna's stomach, then stared at me "Don't ever say I didn't do you any favors, Jack. I'm the one whose ass is hanging in the wind here with the Rojo, and I spent quite an amount of liquid capital tonight, keeping your man alive."

"I appreciate it, but the Rojo were going to screw you anyway. They sent that bloodslave out tonight to meet me at a club and had her offer herself to me."

She frowned. "They fed you? Before a fight? Why?"

"I suspect the word on the street is that I'm a lover not a fighter. They must've thought she'd entertain me, and I'd ditch you." I shrugged, hitching Luna closer, walking back through the club with Maya following me. "They had her prick her finger for me on a rose's thorn and everything. She was an excellent actress, begging me to spend the night and help her spend her sugar daddy's money on caviar."

"Well I'm glad you were able to overcome the temptation of imported fish eggs to help out." Maya said, rounding me to hold open Vermillion's door.

"And I'm glad you were able to keep my man occupied. I do know the risk your people took. Tell them I appreciate it."

"I'll pass it along." I stood in the doorway for a moment, feeling the cold night breeze, listening—*sensing*—for any Good Samaritans that might want to report a heavily tattooed guy carrying a passed out girl to his car to the cops. Finding none, I looked back to Maya. "I'm glad this worked, Maya, but let's not do it again."

She grinned at me, still half-naked and looking feral, her teeth shining in the darkness. "Agreed."

I stepped out into the night and was halfway to my car when I heard her voice behind me. "Hey—Jack. You know he'll come back to you, right?"

I didn't respond to her.

"You're his Master now. He'll have no choice!" she shouted, and then laughed cruelly before I heard the door close and lock.

CHAPTER TWENTY-FOUR
JACK

I drove Luna home and snuck her into my apartment just before dawn, laying her down on the couch and crouching nearby. Her heart beat was slow and I could see what little blood she had coursing through her sluggishly. I knew her current situation was stable but precarious.

I didn't want to call 911—there was no explanation I could give that would be good enough, without endangering myself—but I also didn't want to wake up and find her dead.

Maybe the safest thing was to give her what she'd always wanted —and make Sam have to open up a new vampire file. She'd kept Paco safe and then navigated him to me—I'd never owed someone a bigger debt.

"Luna?" I said, shaking her gently. "Hey, Luna. Don't die on me."

Her dark eyelashes fluttered awake. "What?"

I exhaled a breath I didn't know I was holding as her eyes fought to track me. "You're bad off. I know what you did." There was a bruised spot on the crest of one of her breasts. Offering herself to a fresh vampire must have been terrifying. I stroked her hair out of her face. "I'm ready to give you what you want, Luna. As long as you still want it. Just say it, all right? One more time." I had to hear her say it. After what I did to Paco—I had to be absolutely sure.

Her face lit up with a beatific smile and she beamed at me. "I want to go to the ballet," she said with total conviction, and then fell back asleep.

I didn't know what to make of that. I closed my eyes and then gently kissed her forehead before lifting her up and carrying her into the bedroom to put her in the box with me, taking Paco's empty place.

WILL LUNA TURN AGAINST JACK?
FIND OUT IN BLOOD OF THE DEAD: DARK INK TATTOO BOOK SIX
READ ON FOR A SNEAK PEEK.

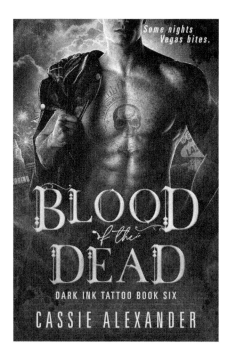

AN EXCERPT FROM BLOOD OF THE DEAD

DARK INK TATTOO BOOK SIX

LUNA

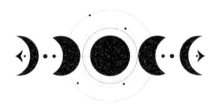

As it turned out, Nilesh only had two condoms, but he'd eaten me out first—and his beard had felt just as fun as I'd thought it would—so I was an orgasm ahead. And our first fuck had just been about us both getting off, but now we wanted to get good.

"Oh, fuck," I groaned. He had my legs splayed wide on the desk, and we were both just watching his rubber-covered cock push into me again. It was even darker than the rest of his skin, and I took some time to marvel at it—I hadn't slept with anyone who was uncircumcised in a long time, it was a shame we couldn't be skin-to-skin.

"Yeah," he agreed, closing his eyes like a cat, feeling the length of him slide inside. I moaned and lay back as far as the desk allowed me, remaining mail scattered everywhere. He was the kind of width that'd make your jaw hurt if you sucked on it for too long—not that I'd have let that stop me from trying, next time I had the chance.

But for right now, he wanted to be inside me, and I wanted that too, feeling his hips roll, as he rocked back and forth. He pulled himself out, played my clit with his cock's head, and then replaced it with his thumb as he sank straight back in.

"I can't believe, all this beautiful skin, and not a singular tattoo," he said, leaning over to kiss my breasts again, playing his tongue across the barbells in my nipples. My shirt was somewhere on the floor beside my panties.

"I still have places you haven't seen," I said, grinning, eyes rolling back, giving myself over to pleasure.

"What, internal organs?" he teased.

I laughed, and he snickered, then he made an animalistic sound, and started fucking me with intent. "Shit, Nilesh," I groaned as he shoved his wide cock home. I slick as hell from already having come twice, but it was like those orgasms had made my walls puffy, and I could feel the thick ridge of the head of his cock as he thrust it inside, riding up into me, before pulling right back down. "God...damn," I panted, and then I reached between my legs, shoving his hand away to replace it with my own. I knew what I wanted and needed, and that was to come, again, around him, and if I managed to come twice before his fat rocket between my legs went off, all the better.

"That's so fucking hot," he growled and grabbed my thighs, hitching me to the edge of the desk, before bending his knees so he could shove himself both in and up inside me.

"Oh, God," I moaned, feeling transported and ready to see in technicolor. "Fuck, fuck, fuck," I called out as touching just the right spot on my clit brought me closer. "Don't stop!" I begged him. "I'm so close!"

He made another snarling sound, like he was tormented by holding his orgasm back.

"I—I—I—" I tried to explain, or warn him, but I couldn't, I just started thrashing on the desk. "Yes!" I shouted, at him, like my master hadn't allowed me to yell at Jack earlier. "Yes, yes, yes!"

Nilesh groaned and rammed himself into me, thrusting wildly, moaning with each fresh jet of cum, and when he was done, he left himself deep, his hips against mine. There was a bead of sweat on his forehead, and I grinned, licking my thumb before reaching up to wipe it off.

"Fuck, Luna," he whispered, slowly pulling out, holding on to the condom as he did so.

"Yeah," I said, trailing a slow hand over my own chest. "Fuck."

Someone beat on the office door from the outside. "You two done in there?"

Nilesh looked guilty, and started hauling his jeans back up. I hopped off the edge of the desk and let my skirt fall, swooping down to grab my shirt. "You didn't lock the door?" I hissed at Nilesh. He raised innocent hands. "Rookie mistake," I mouthed, assembling myself quickly. I pushed him back so that if it was Jack outside, or any other member of Dark Ink's crew, I'd have a chance to explain that what happened in the office that I was newly in charge of was no one else's fucking business.

But instead of any of the semi-strangers I was expecting to see when I whipped open the door, I found a somewhat familiar vampire there, instead.

Paco.

The vampire who'd almost bled me to death, accidentally, a week ago.

"You," I growled, stepping up to face him. His eyes flickered past me, but then realizing I wasn't fucking Jack, he stepped back. "What the hell are you doing here?"

Paco was the definition of tall, dark, and handsome. Strong cheekbones, full lips, and he looked like he could pick up a full slot machine. "No, actually?" I went on. "I know."

Nilesh appeared beside me a moment later and sensed the tension in the air. "Another ex?" he guessed.

"No. It's a long story that I won't tell you sometime—over dinner." I crossed my arms. "But it doesn't concern you."

Nilesh gave me look of concern. "You're sure?"

"Plenty." I managed to give him a tense smile. "Please, go?"

He kept a steady eye on Paco as he finished fastening his belt buckle shamelessly, which I liked, and then dodged around him to head for the door, giving me one look back. I waved him away.

The second the door was closed, Paco gave me a withering stare. "You shouldn't encourage him. He doesn't know what you are."

I went back into the office and picked up my abandoned sports bra and my bag. "A girl's gotta eat, and currently a girl doesn't get paid very well—and we both know Jack doesn't go grocery shopping. Why're you here, Paco?"

"I wanted to talk to Jack."

"Have you tried texts or emails?" I suggested sarcastically.

He frowned. "In person. I figured this was neutral territory."

"Yeah, right." I pulled my backpack on. "What would you have done if it had been him fucking some co-ed inside there?"

Paco's hands curled closed but he didn't say anything. Then he opened his mouth, but I shook my head, fiercely. "Nope. Fuck you. I'm neither of your errand boys. And while I may be his secretary here, I do not take Jack's personal messages." I put my hands on his broad chest and started shoving him towards the door.

Keep reading

Blood of the Dead: Dark Ink Tattoo Book six

And be sure to join Cassie's mailing list for secret scenes, more character art, merchandise, and extra stories!

DARK INK TATTOO SERIES

Don't miss the rest of the Dark Ink Tattoo Series.

...with more to come!

ABOUT THE AUTHOR

Cassie Alexander is a registered nurse and author. She's written numerous paranormal romances, sometimes with her friend Kara Lockharte. She lives in the Bay Area with one husband, two cats, and one million succulents.

ALSO BY CASSIE ALEXANDER

CHECK OUT CASSIEALEXANDER.COM FOR CONTENT/TRIGGER WARNINGS.

THE DARK INK TATTOO SERIES

Blood of the Pack

Blood at Dusk

Blood at Midnight

Blood at Moonlight

Blood at Dawn

Blood of the Dead *(January 2023)*

The Longest Night (Newsletter Bonus Story & Audio)

EDIE SPENCE SERIES

Nightshifted

Moonshifted

Shapeshifted

Deadshifted

Bloodshifted

TRANSFORMATION TRILOGY *(Coming early 2023)*

Bend Her

Break Her

Make Her

STANDALONE STORIES

AITA?

Her Ex-boyfriend's Werewolf Lover

Her Future Vampire Lover

The House

Rough Ghost Lover

WRITTEN WITH KARA LOCKHARTE

THE PRINCE OF THE OTHER WORLDS SERIES

Dragon Called

Dragon Destined

Dragon Fated

Dragon Mated

Dragons Don't Date (Prequel Short Story)

Bewitched (Newsletter Exclusive Bonus Story)

THE WARDENS OF THE OTHER WORLDS SERIES

Dragon's Captive

Wolf's Princess

Wolf's Rogue *(Coming soon)*

Dragon's Flame *(Coming soon)*

Printed in Great Britain
by Amazon

11049851R00098